FREDDY AND THE FRENCH FRIES

FRIES ALIVE!

by David Baldacci
with art by Rudy Baldacci

 LITTLE, BROWN AND COMPANY

New York ᣞ Boston

Little, Brown and Company

Time Warner Book Group
1271 Avenue of the Americas, New York, NY 10020
Visit our Web site at www.lb-kids.com

First Edition: June 2005

Library of Congress Cataloging-in-Publication Data

Baldacci, David.
  Fries alive! / by David Baldacci ; illustrated by Rudy Baldacci.—1st ed.
      p. cm. —(Freddy and the French Fries)
  Summary: While competing with a rival restaurant for the winning float in the Founder's Day parade, nine-year-old Freddy Funkhouser constructs a batch of animated French fries in his secret laboratory that come to life after receiving an enormous jolt of electricity.
  ISBN 0-316-15998-0
    [1. Science—Experiments—Fiction. 2. Inventors—Fiction. 3. Competition (Psychology)—Fiction. 4. French fries—Fiction. 5. Humorous stories.] I. Baldacci, Rudy, ill. II. Title. III. Series: Baldacci, David. Freddy and the French Fries.

PZ7.B18124Fr 2005 [Fic]—dc22   2004015108

10 9 8 7 6 5 4 3 2 1

Q-FF

Printed in the United States of America

The illustrations for this book were done in pen and ink on illustration board.
The text was set in Corona, and the display type is Providence Roman.

To Spencer and Collin, my two favorite Fries.

Table of Contents

FREDDY AND THE FRENCH FRIES

CHAPTER 1

FREDDY FUNKHOUSER

FREDDY T. FUNKHOUSER stood at the door of the Burger Castle and scratched his ear, which was a little difficult since he was wearing a chicken costume. He rubbed his beak and practiced his clucking as he waited for customers. His father, Alfred Funkhouser, insisted that Freddy greet each customer that came into the Funkhouser family's restaurant with a welcoming "cluck-cluck."

"Pow-pow-pow!" said Alfred Funkhouser as he rolled by on skates, dressed in his tomato costume, shooting seeds from the automatic seed shooters attached to his forearms. The seed shooter was one of Alfred's many strange inventions. "Take cover, incoming. Ack-ack-ack!" cried out Alfred as he fired all over the place.

"Better save the ammo for the paying customers, Dad," Freddy said as he patiently picked the tiny seeds off his wings.

"Right-O, Freddy. How many customers have we had today?"

"That would be, like, *zero*," said Freddy's thirteen-year-old sister, Nancy, as she flounced by in her ketchup-bottle costume. An aspiring actress, the tall, skinny Nancy Funkhouser *flounced* dramatically everywhere, swishing her flaming red hair this way and that. She had a large trunk of costumes in her bedroom she had gotten from an old theater and dressed up in crazy outfits all the time. She constantly spouted dialogue from plays, movies, TV, and commercials.

"O Romeo, Romeo, wherefore art thou, Romeo?" cried out Nancy to an invisible audience. The five Guacamole brothers, who worked at the restaurant dressed as French fries, looked up, sniggered, and went back to their card playing and magazine reading.

"Cluck-cluck," replied Freddy, staring at his sister and tapping his beak with his left wing. "Cluck-cluck, here I am, O Nanny Boo-Boo. Herefore art I am."

Freddy and his Dad sometimes called her "Nanny Boo-Boo" because when he was very little, Freddy would run to his big sister when he got hurt and say, "Nanny, Boo-Boo." Even though he was nine years old now, Freddy still called her that when he wanted to make her mad. He considered making his sister miserable one of the most important jobs he had, because she certainly tried to make his life miserable every chance she got.

"Hmmpph," she snorted. "You've ruined my concentration. I can't possibly work under these conditions," she complained.

"You're not working right now," pointed out Freddy.

"Duh. We don't have any customers. They're all over there cramming dead cows into their mouths."

Nancy pointed her bottle top across the street to the enormous and fancy burger restaurant owned by the Spanker family. Patty Cakes, which served everything from burgers to cakes, was far more than a restaurant. The place had its own Ferris wheel, roller coaster, splash rides, movie theater, video arcade, and lots more. Their competitor's sign had a large plastic charcoal hamburger patty sitting on top of a pink cake. The patty and cake logo was on everything, from the staff uniforms to advertisements in the paper to the Patty Cakes blimp that glided all over town. The Spankers drove a big pink Cadillac that played the ditty: "Patty-cake, patty-cake, Spanker man, follow us, follow us to Spanker Land."

It made Freddy want to puke every time he heard it.

"Beef — it's what's for dinner," said Nancy dramatically, and then fell to the floor in a moving death scene before standing and taking a bow. "Thank you, thank you," she murmured.

"No, no encore, really, not another encore, my adoring fans. Fifteen is enough. Well, perhaps just *one* more."

Freddy could only shake his head. Of fifty million sisters he could have had, he got *her*. He said, "I've performed a rigorous calculation and concluded that the fat and sodium content of a number six deluxe special at Patty Cakes is equal to eating four fatted calves and five pounds of salt." Freddy liked to use big words when he talked about scientific stuff.

"Right-o, Freddy," agreed his father. "I've made the same calculation. Not very healthy fare."

"But that's why everyone goes there, Dad," explained his daughter, "because it's bad for you and grease tastes good." She performed a little tap dance and squirted ketchup out of her costume's head. "Good to the last drop," she recited to her adoring fans.

"It doesn't taste half as good as Dad's soybean and tofu burgers or carrot and eggplant hot dogs," Freddy shot back. "Or how about the fat-free fries that make your hair grow?"

Alfred Funkhouser piped in, "And don't forget the Vroom shakes, which increase brain cell function fourteen-and-a-half percent on average, according to my latest tests." He searched the pockets of his tomato costume. "Now where did I put those results?"

"Well, the brussels-sprout-and-cauliflower doughless pizza gave me gas," replied Nancy.

"That's what they invented air fresheners for, dear," said her father.

"What we need," said Freddy, "is to get the word out and let people know about us. The Spankers have commercials all the time on TV, and they have people passing out coupons on all the streets. We should be doing that too."

"You doof! All that costs money — money we don't have," said his sister.

"That's just not fair. Our food is lots better than theirs, and it's good for you too."

"That's why our float in the Founders' Day parade is so important," Alfred said. "It'll help to remind everyone in town about the Burger Castle."

"It'll be the best float ever!" shouted Freddy. "I've been working on something top secret in my lab for it."

"What is it?" asked his father.

"I can't tell you yet, Dad, it's a surprise."

Nancy said, "I thought I'd act out all the plays of Shakespeare while we're driving along the parade route. You know, to give the crowd something really special."

Her father scratched his chin. "All of Shakespeare's plays, Nanny Boo-Boo? Umm, the parade route's not that long."

"Dad, my name's *Nancy*, remember?" she scolded. "Don't worry, I'm going to talk really fast. And you never know; I might even get discovered along the way."

"Discovered? Like by the people from the nuthouse?" piped in Freddy. "Does that mean I can have your room when they take you away in the straitjacket with duct tape over your mouth?"

"Hmmpph," said Nancy as she flounced away with a squirt of ketchup aimed at her little brother.

A few minutes later Freddy walked outside to inspect the Burger Castle sign that hung across the front of the restaurant. The project he was working on for the float competition was based on the sign, and studying the sign helped him think about how the float design should look. The Burger Castle had once been a Laundromat made to look like an old castle complete with drawbridge and turrets. When the Funkhousers bought it, the turrets were sagging like frowning faces and its walls were crumbling. The floors were uneven, the doors didn't open, and there were few windows. It was very dark inside.

The tall, thin Alfred Funkhouser had rubbed his sharp chin as he stared at the grand wreck for the first time. He then whipped out a level and plumb line and, using a thingamabob that looked like something very dangerous if it were thrown at you, he made a calculation. "It's three-quarters of an inch from total collapse. It's perfectly perfect!" he proclaimed, putting a hand through his jet black hair and rubbing a spot off his glasses.

He and the kids spent the next year fixing it up, complete with working drawbridge, a Vroom shake moat encircling it, and painted pickle chips hugging the turrets. No other restaurant in America looked quite like the Burger Castle. Freddy loved it. And yet almost no one ever came to eat there unless it was by accident.

But the project he was now working on for the Burger Castle float would change all that. He looked at the sign again. On either side of the words "Burger" and "Castle" were big French fries. In his secret lab, Freddy had constructed giant Fries using his father's super-secret potatoes. Then he gave them faces, painted them fun colors, and rigged them with wires and a small battery so that with a press of a button they would wave their hands and bob their heads while they were on the float. He had even thought of a way, using a loudspeaker and an electronic gizmo he'd built, to make the Fries appear to be talking. They would tell everyone to come to the Burger Castle. With the addition of the talking Fries, and some other things Freddy was working on, he thought they would be a lock to win the float competition.

Freddy's dream was to become a famous scientist, like his father had been. Alfred Funkhouser had worked for the U.S. Government and won lots of awards for his work. But after Freddy's mother passed away when Freddy was three years old, his father left his job and moved them to the farm so he could spend more time with his children. Freddy believed that his father should still be a big-shot scientist in Washington, D.C., but if his father couldn't be, then Freddy would do it for him.

Freddy looked over at Patty Cakes again, and then at the big warehouse that the Spankers owned next to their restaurant. Even from here Freddy could hear the sounds of machinery, sawing, and hammering. He watched as a big forklift carried a large wooden thing into the warehouse. Curious, Freddy slipped off his chicken costume and sneaked across the street to the warehouse.

A side door to the building was slightly ajar, so Freddy peered in. What he saw made his heart sink. In the middle of the warehouse it looked like they were building a replica of the Patty Cakes. Dozens of workers were hammering, nailing, painting, and sawing. The thing that Freddy had seen the forklift bring in was part of the Ferris wheel. It was now being lowered onto one end of the float. For that's what this was,

Freddy was convinced: the Patty Cake float for the Founders' Day parade.

In a far corner Freddy saw Stewie Spanker, the owner of Patty Cakes, and also the town of Pookesville's police chief *and* mayor, talking with a well-dressed, short, blond-haired man with a skinny mustache whom Freddy had never seen before. They were going over what looked to be plans for the float.

A depressed Freddy walked back to the Burger Castle and put his chicken costume on. They didn't have a chance against the Spanker float. All the work he'd done was worthless. Colorful Fries that smiled and bobbed their heads and said stupid things? Who cared?

SPLAT!

"Ow!" Freddy cried out, and grabbed his arm that had just turned red. He looked over and paled.

Coming across the drawbridge was Adam Spanker and his gang of bullies. They had their fancy paintball guns and wore Army helmets and camouflage uniforms and big black boots.

Adam Spanker had been Freddy's worst nightmare for years. One of his legs was larger than Freddy's chest. His stomach was so big that it was rumored he had actually swallowed a whole person. His hair was cut so short he looked bald.

Some kids at school said Adam's mother was a witch who had taken all his hair when he was born and used it to make poisons. Other kids said that Adam had green blood — a sure sign of a monster.

"Cluck-cluck, Funky Funkhouser!" roared Adam Spanker.

Freddy's teeth chattered uncontrollably. "Yo . . . you're . . . you're tre . . . tress . . . tresspa . . . passing," said Freddy.

"We . . . we . . . we're tre . . . tre . . . tresspa . . . trespassing?" mimicked Adam. "Well, I just saw *you* poking around *our* place, Funky."

"I wasn't doing anything."

"Yeah, right." Adam looked slyly at his gang. "Well, boys, now that we're here, we might as well go into the old burger dump."

"But you never buy anything. And I . . . I . . . think . . ." Freddy stopped.

"Just spit it out, you little nerd," bellowed Adam.

Freddy swallowed a big lump in his throat and said quickly, "I think you're just coming here to engage in clandestine operations with a subversive purpose."

Adam looked totally confused until one of his gang whispered in his ear.

Adam marched up to Freddy towering over him. "Are you calling me a spy?" he snarled.

Freddy looked around at all the big kids with

paint guns staring at him, and his teeny bit of courage melted right away and into the Vroom shake moat. "Well, yes, I mean, no, I, uh, I mean, uh —"

"You got something you want to say to me, say it man to man, Funky," yelled Spanker, his big hands balled into fists.

Freddy desperately wanted to be brave and stand up to Adam, and he would have, except he was scared to death. "Uh, I ... I said ... cluck-cluck, welcome to the Burger Castle."

Adam pointed his paintball gun at Freddy.

"Welcome to the Burger Castle *what*?"

"Uh, welcome to the Burger Castle ... Mr. Spanker?"

"That's better. Come on, men, let's check out the burger dump." As he passed by Freddy, Spanker shot out a big, doughy hand and pushed Freddy into the moat. The gang roared with laughter and then swarmed into the Burger Castle.

Freddy swam to the side of the moat and got out. He wrung his chicken feathers dry and hurried into the Burger Castle to see what the Spanker gang was up to. Turns out they were up to a lot.

"Stop that right now!" yelled Nancy before she was hit in the face by a blue paint splotch. She raised both her hands up and said in a loud, deep voice, "Whosoever shall smite me with another blow shall reap the unstoppable force of all that is good and right."

Then she was smote with a purple paint splotch right in the nose and dove behind the sales counter screaming, "I shall live to fight another day!"

The Guacamole Brothers had scattered when the Spanker gang had attacked. On their way out the back door they yelled in unison, "We quit!"

Alfred rolled out of the back in his tomato costume and said, "Now, you boys stop that right now or I'll be forced to call the chief of police."

Adam shot Alfred in the butt with a green paint splotch.

"Go ahead and call him," crowed Adam. "My *Dad's* right across the street at our warehouse. I'm sure he'll be right over."

Freddy snuck in the side door and started edging toward Adam. Right before he reached him Adam whirled around and drilled him with a shot. Freddy went flying backward, pink paint all over his beak.

Adam and his gang stood triumphantly over their fallen foes. "Look, Funkies," he said, "If I were you I'd just pack up and leave town. Nobody comes to your crummy burger dump and nobody comes to the crummy farm you live on. There's only room for one burger restaurant in this town. And that's the Patty Cakes."

"Oh yeah?" said Nancy. "Just wait until we win the float competition at the Founders' Day parade. Then we'll see who's number one."

Adam laughed. "We've won it five years in a row, and there's nothing stopping us from number six. So the day you win the float competition is the day I turn fat and ugly."

"Gee," said Nancy as she poked her head over the sales counter where she was hiding. "Why don't you just declare us the winner then?"

Adam looked at her in confusion until one of his gang whispered to him.

Adam yelled out to Nancy, "Hey, did you just call me fat and ugly?"

"If the adjectives fit, oh meat-headed one," she said.

Adam looked at his gang. "All right, boys, time to show the Funkies who's boss. Let's give 'em the Deadly Dose." The gang loaded fresh paintball bullets marked with skulls and crossbones in their guns and pointed them at the ceiling.

"Don't!" yelled Alfred. He shot tomato seeds at them, but they bounced harmlessly off the gang.

"Aim!" said Adam.

"Stop!" screamed Nancy, squirting ketchup at them. Adam just licked it off his shirt.

"Fire!!"

"NOOOO!" Freddy tried to run away, but his foot hit some wet paint on the floor and he flipped up in the air, directly in front of the paintball guns as they fired. The paintballs hit him at the same time, covered him with a black ooze, and sent him flying up, up, up to the ceiling.

"Retreat, men!" barked Adam. "Mission accomplished."

The Spanker gang flew out the door.

Alfred and Nancy watched Freddy shooting to the ceiling. He seemed to be moving in slow motion, his mouth open and one long scream coming out of it. "AAAAAHHHHHH!"

When Freddy hit the ceiling of the Burger Castle, the black, sticky ooze rained down all over the restaurant.

BAM! Freddy hit the floor and lay there. He slowly sat up and looked at his father and sister. Covered in black, they all looked like they had just struck oil.

"And stay out," whispered Freddy to the long-gone Adam Spanker and his gang.

"Well," said Alfred as he wiped the black off his glasses. "Those boys certainly are mischievous."

"Mischievous?" exclaimed Nancy. "They should be in prison."

"Now, Nanny Boo-Boo," replied her father.

"Maybe we *should* leave town, Dad," said Nancy. "Adam's father owns the Patty Cakes, *and* he's the police chief, *and* the mayor. We don't stand a chance. And I'm running out of clothes that don't have paint splotches on them."

Freddy said angrily, "We're not going to let Spanker and his gang run us out of town. Right, Dad?"

"Well, if we don't start getting customers coming in soon, Freddy, the decision won't be up to us. We won't be able to afford to stay here. We don't have much savings left."

"Don't worry, Dad, our float will win and this place will be packed."

"I hope so," answered his father.

"We *will* win," said Freddy. But he wasn't nearly as confident as he sounded.

As they were driving home that evening, Freddy fell asleep in the back of the station wagon. He dreamt that the Funkhousers had won the float competition and the Burger Castle was crammed with customers, and that he was big and strong and had just beaten up Adam and his whole gang all by himself. But when he woke up he was still Freddy Funkhouser, a nine-year-old boy who was small for his age, wore glasses, and had blond hair that always stuck up in back.

Freddy couldn't use his brawn to beat Spanker since he didn't have any. But he did have something Spanker didn't have: A brain. A big one!

"Think, Freddy, think." And then it hit him. He almost yelled out, he was so excited. He had the very thing that would win the competition and finally beat the Spankers and their fancy float.

When they got home Freddy raced to his secret laboratory.

"This means war, Adam Spanker," he called out as he sprinted there. "And you're going down or my name isn't Freddy Tesla Funkhouser."

CHAPTER 2

THE FUNKHOUSER EXPERIMENT

Freddy had spent the last week reworking the special project he was doing for the Burger Castle float. Exhausted, he now leaned against the wall of his laboratory. His lab was underneath one of the old barns on the farm he and his family lived on. Over the last few years Freddy had outfitted his lab with leftover equipment and machinery he had found on the farm. The large room was crammed with inventions he had built from old tractors, generators, combines, tillers, lawnmowers, milking machines, and tons of other stuff. He had done many experiments, first under the close eye of his father, but now he did a lot by himself. His father had taught him that a good scientist thought through all the consequences before conducting an experiment. Well, Freddy had given his latest project a lot of thought and work, but he still had a big problem.

There was a loud buzzing sound and Freddy picked up an old phone that was attached to a black cord.

"Who is it?"

"Howie," said the voice on the phone.

"What's the password?" Freddy said.

"Adam Spanker eats his own boogers," said the voice.

"Roger that," answered Freddy.

"Over and out," said the voice.

Freddy hit a button on his big lab table. There was a scream and something dropped from the ceiling and landed in a pile of hay behind him.

Howie Kapowie stood unsteadily and brushed the straw off his clothes. He was one of Freddy's friends. Actually, Howie was Freddy's *only* friend. Howie was even smaller than Freddy, with brown hair that had an even bigger cowlick than Freddy's. He looked unhappily at his chum. "I thought you were going to work out the kinks on the trapdoor. I've got straw in my underwear."

"I've been too busy, Howie," said a weary Freddy. "I've been working on this experiment every night for the last week."

Howie pulled out a cheese cube from his pocket and popped it in his mouth. Howie loved cheese cubes more than anything. "What kind of experiment?"

"Well, I'm trying to make something really special for our Founders' Day float."

"But the Spankers win every year."

"I know. Their float's pretty awesome this year," admitted Freddy. "I snuck a peek in their warehouse. There was some strange man in there talking with Chief Spanker."

"Knowing the Spankers they probably hired him to build it for them."

"The rules say you have to build your own."

"The Spankers make their own rules, you know that."

Freddy sighed, but then looked excited. "Can you keep a secret?"

Howie looked offended. "I'm a Kapowie; we're very trustworthy people."

"This is a super top-secret secret of the highest order."

"Does the fate of the entire world hang in the balance?"

"Quite possibly."

Howie popped another cheese cube in his mouth. "Okay, I'm cool with that. Let me have it, Freddio."

Freddy led him over to a door, opened it, and went into a small room. Howie followed him. It was very dark.

"I can't see anything," said Howie.

"The lights automatically come on when the door's closed."

Freddy shut the door and the whole room lit up.

"AAAAHHHHH!!!" screamed Howie Kapowie, and he fainted.

Freddy looked down at his friend. "Howie? Howie?" Freddy shook his head, reached in Howie's pocket, pulled out a cheese cube, and held it under his friend's nose.

Howie's nostrils started quivering as they sucked in the smell of the cheese. Finally, Howie's tongue shot out, scooped up the cheese cube, and his eyes opened and he sat up.

"What is THAT?" he asked, pointing.

"I made them for the float. And I thought we could use them as the symbol for the Burger Castle. You know, like Patty Cakes has. Only lots better."

Howie stood and peered at the figures lined up against the wall. There were five of them, and all except one were a lot taller than Freddy. They sort of looked like French fries, but they were painted bright colors with faces, arms, and legs. The blue one had on a bowtie and wore thick black glasses. The green one wore a baseball cap. The purple one was the biggest of all with a big butt and belly. The yellow one was the smallest, but had really huge eyes and mouth. One half of the red one's face was smiling, the other half was frowning.

Freddy explained. "At first I just made them out of my Dad's secret potatoes and wired them so they could do a few movements. But after seeing the Spanker float I knew I needed something a lot cooler than that. So I used microchips from some old computers to hardwire their brains. I used the biggest microchip I had in the blue one. I call him Theodore. The purple one is Wally, because he's in the shape of a waffle fry. The chip in his brain got damaged, but I figured it would still work. The yellow one is Ziggy. I gave him a very funny feature." He pointed to the green Fry. "That's Curly,

21

because he's a curlicue Fry. He can stretch twenty feet into the air, although I had some problems wiring his voice box."

"So they can talk?" asked an amazed Howie.

"Well, that's the general idea. The red Fry I don't have a name for yet. I split its brain chip in half and did some special wiring to give it two different personalities. I thought it'd be kind of neat."

Howie timidly walked over and gently touched the purple Fry's leg.

"What are they made of?"

"That's the best part. Like I said, I used my dad's super secret potatoes, but I reinforced them with carbon tubes bonded together. Carbon tubing is stronger than anything else in the universe and it's more flexible than rubber or plastic. It's called nanotechnology. My dad worked on it when he was with the government. I also built in an electronic-based nervous system and aluminum skeletal platform."

"Does your dad know you used his stuff?"

Freddy looked a little nervous. "Uh, I haven't exactly told him yet. I just sort of borrowed the nanotechnology formula and added the potatoes and a few things of my own. I'm sure he won't mind."

"So, how come they're not talking or moving?"

"That's the problem. I discovered that the

energy source required to jump-start them is huge, at least a million jiggy-watts of power. I don't have anywhere near enough in my generator. I don't know what I'm going to do," he added glumly as he sat on the floor.

Howie sat next to Freddy. "A million jiggy-watts, huh? Heck, the hydroelectric dam where my dad works only has half that much power."

Freddy looked at his friend. "But aren't there *two* dams—an upper and a lower one?"

"Yeah, so?"

"So they each produce half-a-million jiggy-watts?"

"Yeah?"

Freddy said excitedly, "Well, the last time I checked, 500,000 plus 500,000 equals a million."

"But how are you going to use the dam's power to fire up the Fries?"

"I know just how, but I'm going to need your help. It could be dangerous, though."

Howie paled. "Gee, Freddy, I don't know."

"Are you my best friend?"

"I'm your only friend."

"Okay, so are you a man or a mouse?"

Howie pulled out a handful of cheese cubes. "Squeak-squeak," he said.

"Listen, Howie, if we pull this off, we'll be world-famous. That's always been my dream. We'll meet the president, for gosh sakes. We'll even go to

Disney World." Howie didn't look impressed with any of this.

"Gee whiz, Howie, what will it take for you to help me?"

Howie thought for a bit and then said, "The world's largest cheese cube is at a museum in Paris. It's made from the world's most stinky cheese, Pâté du Pooty; it's a hundred feet high and weighs eight and a half tons."

"It's yours."

"Let's go get those jiggy-watts."

CHAPTER 3

THE JIGGY-WATTS CAPER

"Freddy, are you really sure this is a good idea?" shouted Howie.

"It's the only way that I can see to do it," Freddy yelled back.

It was very early the next morning. They both had sneaked out of their houses to go on this very special mission. They were on the Pookesville Lake, steering their raft closer to the top of the Pookesville Dam. Piled under a tarp on the raft were the five Fries and some special equipment that Freddy had brought.

Howie looked at the dark sky. "Looks like a storm's coming in."

"I checked the weather forecast. We should be long gone before it hits."

The raft touched a stone barrier at the side of the dam and the boys tied up there.

"Okay, Howie, there're the stairs to the control room. That's where the turbines are, right?"

"Yep. And there's no one there right now. My dad doesn't get in until nine."

"You got the key?"

Howie held it up. "The spare from my Dad's desk at home."

"Roger that."

"Over and out, up and down. BINGO!" yelled an excited Howie.

They carried the Fries and equipment down the stairs and to the control room. Howie unlocked the door and they went in.

"Wow," said Freddy, looking around at all the shiny equipment. "This is so cool."

"Yeah, and it's got almost as much stuff as your lab."

"Okay, let's go. I'll re-program the control board to divert the necessary power from the hydroelectric operations to the Fries for one-point-two milliseconds. According to my calculations, that should be all that we need."

While Freddy reprogrammed the controls, Howie hooked up electrodes to each of the Fries and then attached these by cables to the massive turbines where the electricity gathered from the dam was collected.

They heard a rumble of thunder outside.

"Wow, that storm is really moving fast," observed Howie as he looked out the window.

"You ready, Howie?" asked Freddy as he finished pushing buttons.

"Ready."

Freddy and Howie put on safety goggles and lead vests and moved behind a wall. In his hand Freddy held a small remote. "Okay, Howie, keep your fingers crossed."

"Finger, toes, but don't pick your nose," recited Howie, who took a deep breath and closed his eyes. Freddy took his own deep breath, and hit the button.

At first nothing happened and Freddy thought something had gone wrong.

But then there was a low humming sound, and then a louder one, and then an enormous *CRRAAACCCKKK!* This was followed by a blinding flash of light. And then there was a burning smell. And then everything became quiet again.

Freddy slowly opened his eyes and looked around the corner.

The Fries were still there, their heads still attached to the electrodes. However, other than being slightly singed, nothing had changed. They were still lumps of lifeless potato and carbon.

Freddy stared at his remote control. "We hit them with a million jiggy-watts and it didn't work. I . . . I can't believe it."

Howie looked at his watch. "We better get going. My dad will be here soon."

They packed up their gear and the Fries and carried them back out to the raft.

"What am I gonna do, Howie?" muttered a

depressed Freddy. "This was my last chance."

"Here, have a cheese cube. It'll make you think better."

The boys put on their life jackets, and while Freddy chewed on his cheese cube Howie steered their raft back out onto the lake.

"Better start paddling, Freddy," barked Howie. "That storm is right on top of us."

Freddy started paddling halfheartedly. But then the wind picked up. The waves got bigger and the rain started falling hard like millions of BBs. Then Freddy started paddling really fast.

Howie's face grew very pale. "Uh, Freddy?"

"Yeah?"

"Is that what I think it is?"

Freddy looked to where Howie was pointing. A wave ten feet high was bearing down on them fast.

"AAAAHHHH!!!" both boys screamed together.

"Abandon ship," yelled Howie.

"What about the Fries?" screamed Freddy over the claps of thunder.

"We can always make more. But there's only two of us."

Both boys jumped in the water and swam for their lives. Freddy looked back as he was swimming. The raft was heading right for the big wave.

"Fries!" screamed Freddy. He turned around in the water and started swimming toward the raft, but the current was so strong that the raft was

pulling farther and farther away from him.

At that instant a bolt of lightning so big it looked like a wall of electricity coming down from the heavens hit the raft full force. A split second later the wave washed over the Fries, pushing the inflatable raft underneath the water. There were no more Fries. There was no more anything.

And then the wave kept on coming, right at Freddy!

"Swim, Freddy, swim!" called out Howie, who was already on the shore and waving to his friend.

Freddy took one last look at where the Fries had been and then turned and swam as fast as he could. But still the wave grew closer and closer.

Howie danced along the shoreline, waving his hands and yelling, "Swim, SWIM!" He was so scared he kept stuffing cheese cubes in his mouth between screams.

But Freddy couldn't swim any faster than he was. The wave was now twenty feet high and right on top of him.

"NOOOO!" screamed Howie.

"NNOOOOO!" yelled Freddy even louder.

The wave crashed right on top of Freddy.

Howie stuffed all his remaining cheese cubes in his mouth, swallowed, and then passed out.

CHAPTER 4

SIX FRIES IF YOU COUNT HEADS

Freddy felt himself being pushed down, down, down into the cold grip of the water.

Oh boy, he thought, *I've really done it now. If I survive this, Dad's gonna kill me.*

Then something grabbed Freddy and propelled him to the surface so fast that it felt like he was on a rocket. He exploded out of the water, and kept going up, up, up. . . . And then he was going down, down, down. And he landed on something very soft and very warm.

"Is he dead?" said a voice.

"Nah, he's going to be just fine, better than fine, absolutely *terrific* in fact," exclaimed a very happy-sounding voice.

"I'm sure he's dead," said a gloomy voice.

"Why do you say that?" asked another voice.

"Because nothing good has ever happened to me, that's why," replied the gloomy voice.

Freddy finally managed to open his eyes. Now he knew he was dead.

All he could see were colors, swirling colors,

right before his eyes. It was pretty, but sort of nauseating at the same time. He sat up, his eyes still not focused. He rubbed them but he still saw rainbows of color.

"I told you he was alive," chirped the happy voice.

"Hey, what's going on up there?" bellowed a deep voice.

A very authoritative voice declared, "I believe that the young man will fully recover posthaste. There seems to be no permanent damage done and all neuromuscular systems appear to be functioning normally."

"Yeah, but is he going to be *okay*?" asked the deep voice.

Freddy's eyes finally focused and he gaped.

Five—no, six faces and ten—no, twelve eyeballs looked back at him.

Freddy screamed. And then *they* screamed. And then Freddy smiled, really, really big. He was excited, not scared. They were his Fries, and they had come to life! There was Ziggy, the yellow Fry, and Theodore, the blue Fry, and Curly, the green Fry, and . . . He stared at the red Fry. It had *two* heads and only one body. Freddy started jumping up and down.

"I did it! I did it!" he yelled.

"Hey, that tickles," said the deep voice.

Freddy looked under his feet and saw that the

thing he was standing on was purple. He raced to the side of whatever they were on and looked over.

"Hey, there," said the deep voice.

Freddy was standing on the purple Fry's enormous stomach.

"How'd you make yourself into a raft?" asked Freddy.

"I'm not sure. It just seemed like a good idea, and then it just happened."

Freddy beamed. "Potato-nanotechnology — you just can't beat it." Freddy held on tight as the storm passed over them, rocking the purple boat and soaking them with rain.

Freddy rubbed his eyes clear and looked over to shore and saw Howie lying there. "Hey, Howie, are you okay?" he yelled.

Howie slowly came to, looked at the Fries, and promptly fainted again.

Freddy felt a tug on his shirt.

"What were you doing at the bottom of the lake?" asked the small yellow Fry.

"I was trying to bring you to life and got hit by a big wave." They looked at him in confusion. "You see, you're my Fries," said Freddy. "I made you."

The blue Fry adjusted his thick glasses that made him look very smart. "You created us? How very interesting."

"And you each have lots of special features," Freddy continued.

The blue Fry smiled knowingly. "I myself feel quite brilliant."

"I just feel hungry," moaned the purple Fry, and the floor moved under their feet. "There, did you hear that rumbling? I have to eat forty-three-and-a-half times a day just to sustain my present figure."

"But I don't understand . . . I thought my experiment failed," said a confused Freddy. "The million jiggy-watts wasn't enough —" Just then there was another flash of lightning. And then Freddy realized what had happened.

"The lightning bolt that hit the raft must have had lots more electricity than a million jiggy-watts. *That* must have brought you to life."

Wow, thought Freddy. *This is the greatest experiment ever. This is history!* I'll be famous! And this might only be the beginning. I'll be on the cover of every magazine; I'll be on TV. And if I get really, really famous, I might even have my own cartoon show. . . .

He was lightheaded with the possibilities. Serious and important people would ask him things like, "Now, Dr. Funkhouser, what is your view on the state of the world, sir?" And he'd say something clever like, "Well, Mr. Ambassador, I personally think a ton of chocolate chip cookies in every household would improve the state of the world. That and duct-taping the mouths of every big sister in America."

"You mean to say," said the blue Fry, "that the lightning bolt interacted with us, causing a reaction of enormous kinetic energy, and now we have discernible motor and intellectual skills as a result of this spontaneous elemental combustion?"

"Yes," shouted Freddy gleefully.

"Wow," said the purple Fry. "And here I thought that big spark that fried my butt had made us come to life."

"And I named you too," added Freddy breathlessly.

The little yellow Fry looked up and asked in an excited voice, "What's my name?"

"You're Ziggy."

The yellow Fry swelled up and his face contorted into something really frightening. "ZIGGY!" cried the yellow Fry so loudly that the air coming out of his mouth made Freddy's hair stick straight up.

Freddy looked at the small Fry fearfully. "Don't you like it?"

The yellow Fry returned to normal size and smiled pleasantly. "Oh, I think it's really swell, thanks."

Freddy swallowed nervously. How could Ziggy go from furious to nice so quickly? Had he miswired the yellow Fry's brain?

"And me?" asked the tall blue Fry. "What's my moniker?"

"You're Theodore," said Freddy. "And you're Wally," he said, leaning over the side of the purple raft.

Wally smiled and then started drinking part of the lake. "I need lots of liquid in my diet," he explained. "It guards against, you know, that poop backup thingie."

"You're referring to constipation," said Theodore.

Wally nodded and his eyes grew huge as he said in a low voice, "Right. Constantinople is bad, very, very bad."

"And us?" said one of the two redheads.

"Hmmm," said a puzzled Freddy. "I hadn't given you names. And there used to be only *one* of you."

The unhappy-looking redhead's mouth drooped even more and his eyes were downcast. "Oh, it's okay. I probably don't deserve a name anyway."

The other redhead was smiling broadly and looked ready to laugh at any moment. He smacked his twin on the back. "Hey, I bet he'll come up with a great name for us. Uh, names, that is." He looked at Freddy. "You will, won't you?"

Freddy looked very uncomfortable for a moment, but then it hit him. He had split the wiring on the chip in the red Fry's head to give it

36

two personalities. When the Fry had separated into two heads, each had taken one of the personalities: sad and happy.

"I've got it," he exclaimed. He pointed to the smiling redhead. "You're Si." He pointed to the depressed redhead. "And you're Meese." He laughed. "Get it? Sia — meese?"

Si and Meese looked clueless.

"Siamese twins," said Theodore in his authoritative voice. "The pairing of identical persons within one body. Decidedly rare indeed. Although I believe the more modern term is 'conjoined.'"

"Hey," pouted Wally, "I was just about to say that."

"But *con* and *joined* just don't have the same ring as Si and Meese," said Freddy.

"Rare, huh?" said Si. "Wow, I told you he'd come up with a great one. That'a boy, Freddy."

Meese looked even more depressed. "If it's so rare I bet no one will remember it."

Freddy looked over at the green Fry that was staring at him from under his ball cap, but then the Fry quickly looked away. Freddy said, "Don't you want to know what your name is?"

The green Fry shook its head, but he did turn one anxious eyeball in Freddy's direction. "You're a curlicue fry, so I named you Curly."

Curly looked like he wanted to smile but didn't exactly know how. So instead he blew his nose very loudly and wiggled his enormous ears.

"Good job, Curly," Freddy said. "You're a good nose blower and ear wiggler."

"Thankyouverymuch," mumbled Curly.

"And what's your name?" asked Theodore.

"Freddy. Freddy T. Funkhouser."

"What's the T stand for?" asked Theodore.

"Tesla. He was a very famous inventor. My dad's an inventor too."

"Cool, what does he invent?" said Wally. "Uh, what's *invent* mean?"

"To construct something of originality using one's imagination and know-how," said Theodore.

"Hey, you're an inventor, Freddy, because you invented us," exclaimed Ziggy.

"That's right!" said Freddy. "In fact, I'm well on my way to being the most famous inventor ever." A crack of lightning hit near them. "But right now we need to get to shore, fast."

"No problem, little dude," said Wally. He turned his mouth to the water and started blowing. The purple raft shot toward land.

Freddy's mind was going a million miles a minute. He could see now that simply sticking the Fries on the Burger Castle float was kid stuff. Very soon everyone would know them. And he and his dad would be famous together. They wouldn't need the Burger Castle to make a living.

He turned to the Fries. "I need time to think of the best way to introduce you to the world. So until then, you have to stay hidden."

The Fries all looked at each other, and finally Theodore said in his deep voice, "You have our solemn word that we will henceforth remain incognito."

"Yep, incockadoodle," added Wally.

When they reached land, Freddy poured some water on Howie's face to revive him. Howie sat up, and Freddy quickly introduced him to the Fries.

"You did it, Freddy!" yelled an excited Howie.

Freddy was beaming. "Yep. The Fries are officially alive."

CHAPTER 5

THE FLIGHT OF THE FRIES

By the time they got back to the barn that was on top of Freddy's secret lab the storm had passed and the day was turning warm and sunny. Reminding the Fries to stay hidden in the barn, the boys left to go home and get ready for school.

The Fries did keep their word about staying out of sight — until Wally got hungry and slipped outside to look for food, only to fall asleep. That wouldn't have been a big problem except that Nancy Funkhouser, who'd left school early that day because she said she wasn't feeling well, chose that time to slink out of bed and go swimming in the small pond near Freddy's secret laboratory.

After she finished her swim, Nancy decided to pick some flowers while she dried off. Next to Freddy's lab there was a whole bunch of pretty ones. One by one she plucked them — reds and yellows and blues and — and then she saw a fat purple one. And it had five toes attached to it! She touched it and it moved. She jumped back. She touched it again and it moved again, and then she thought she heard a giggle.

"Who's that?" she said in a frightened voice.

Wally sat straight up from where he had been taking a nap in the flowers.

"It's me, Wally," he boomed out. Then he looked panicked. "Oops, I wasn't supposed to let you see me. But since you're here, do you have anything to eat?" He grabbed the flowers she was holding and swallowed them. "Nice appetizer. Can I see the dinner menu now?"

A screaming Nancy ran off so fast her red hair stuck straight out behind her; it looked like her head was on fire.

That scared Wally so badly he took off running too, and ran right into the barn door and knocked himself out. He lay on the ground, a great big purple blob.

The other Fries peeked out of the barn and saw Nancy running off.

"My educated opinion," said Theodore, "is that we have been discovered."

"I bet they'll come and eat us," added Meese sadly. "And I just got my name too. Even if nobody will ever remember it."

"We have to hide," squeaked Ziggy.

"I bet we'll find a great place to hide," responded Si. "A super-duper swello one. Right, Meese?"

"We're all doomed," replied Meese gloomily. "We'll be crushed to bits. We probably only have seconds to live. Oh, well — it's not like anyone will miss me."

"Yeah, but they'll miss *me*. I'm a real fun guy to be around," exclaimed Si. "And if you go down, *I* go down."

At that moment, Curly uncoiled himself so he was about twelve feet tall. He saw the two people coming over the hill. He tapped Theodore on the shoulder.

"Ohboygottamovefastpeoplecoming," he mumbled hurriedly.

"Let's expedite our removal from these environs with all due haste," ordered an alarmed Theodore.

"NO TIME FOR THAT, LET'S RUN!" shouted Wally, who had woken up and heard Curly.

The Fries shot into the woods in such a blur of color that they looked like a running rainbow.

Minutes later, Nancy came sprinting up holding a large frying pan in one hand and a can of bug killer in the other. Her father came puffing up behind her. His head and hands were bandaged. "Okay, Nanny Boo-Boo, where are they, whatever they are?"

She sputtered, "They — it — that *thing* was right here. Right here!" She swung her frying pan around, and sprayed the bug spray. The only thing that did was to scare off a bunch of butterflies.

"Now stop that, dear, you'll hurt yourself."

Nancy kept swinging and spraying. "*Me* hurt *myself*? *You* blew yourself up again. You know, Dad, most people make waffles without a steam iron and a blowtorch."

"How very unexciting. Now what was it you saw again?"

"A huge purple blobby thing. It was deee-ssssggusting, it really was. It had toes. And a big purple tongue. And two beady little purple eyes. And it spoke to me. It said its name was Wally."

"That's nice," her father began, and then he stopped abruptly. "I thought you were sick in bed. What were you doing out here?"

"Why, of course I'm sick," Nancy said as she quickly tried to think of something. "That's why I *believed* I saw a purple fry, which of course is silly. I better go and lie down. I'm feeling faint." She dropped the frying pan and bug spray, put her hand to her forehead, and started spinning around. "Everything's getting dizzy and dark, Dad. I think it's my time, my time to go to the great here-after." She started shivering. "So cold, so cold." She dropped to her knees and started to moan. "Are you still there, Dad? It's okay if you're not. I can die all alone. Really. Oh, E.T. phone home, one last time, E.T., one final time," she said tearfully. She swooned three times, gave a little gasp, clutched her chest, and then fell to the grass and lay still.

Her father stared down at her, rubbing his sharp chin. "You probably just caught a bug. I'm going to give you a big spoonful of my special medicine. I just made a fresh batch out of rutabagas and extract of poppy seed oil with a pinch of jalapeno and just a dab of limburger cheese to open your sinuses. It's a wonderfully wondrous concoction. And not only does it make me feel better, but I can also see out the back of my head, which is quite useful actually for a parent."

Nancy sat up and looked terrified. "No, Dad, please! Remember the last time? My hair hasn't grown all the way back, and one ear's still bigger than the other."

"Don't worry, I've worked those bugs out. You know that safety comes first with me."

Nancy looked at her dad's bandaged head and hands and muttered, "Right."

As they walked off she said to herself, "I just know this is all Freddy's doing. And I'm *so* going to get him back. Freddy Funkhouser, you are like sooooo in trouble."

CHAPTER 6

THE WORLD'S MOST FAMOUS KID

Freddy was so excited about becoming famous that he floated through most of his classes that day. He didn't answer a single question asked of him, or if he did, the answer was wrong.

"No, Freddy, Bugs Bunny was not the first president of the United States," said his history teacher. "No, six times seven is not a cheeseburger with fries," said his math teacher.

Freddy was so distracted that he put his finger in the pencil sharpener and stapled his shirt to his desk. And at lunch he ate the wax paper his sandwich was wrapped in rather than the meatless bologna sandwich his father had made for him.

Howie Kapowie had been watching Freddy all day. At lunch, when Freddy stuck his milk straw in his nose and tried to inhale, Howie Kapowie asked him what was wrong.

But Freddy wasn't listening. He was daydreaming about being interviewed on TV as the world's most famous person. He had just been asked what he was going to do now that he had accomplished the greatest feat in world history.

Suddenly, Freddy jumped on the lunchroom table, thrust his fist in the air, and shouted, "I'm going to Disney World. YYYYEEEAAAHHH!"

When Freddy remembered where he was, he looked at everybody staring at him. Howie had been startled so badly that he had stuck a cheese cube in his right ear. Adam Spanker glared at him from another table and laughed. So did all his gang.

"Funky Funkhouser, you're such a loser," yelled Adam. "I wish you'd go to outer space where you belong." The gang all rolled with laughter.

Freddy climbed down from the table after

pulling his feet free from Darcella Macomber's mashed potatoes and gravy. "Uh, sorry," he said to Darcella.

"Freak!" she exclaimed before storming out.

"Uh, are you okay, Freddy?" asked Howie as he tried to get the cheese cube out of his ear. He didn't like to waste his cheese cubes.

"I can't stop thinking about the Fries, Howie. It's a pretty overwhelming concept. There'll be all the press coverage, meeting the president and other world leaders, touring the globe, the awards and medals, money pouring in, making statues of me around the world, and then the excitement will really start."

"But, Freddy, I thought you made the Fries so that your family would win the Founders' Day parade and save the Burger Castle," Howie pointed out.

Freddy looked at him like he was crazy. "Sure, that was the original plan, but that's small potatoes, Howie. I have to think bigger now. I'm talking the *world*, not some crummy parade."

"But if you don't put the Fries on the Burger Castle float the Spankers will win for sure."

"Who cares? My family won't even be living in Pookesville much longer."

"Where will you go?"

"Who knows? New York, Paris, London, maybe even Hollywood."

"Hollywood?"

"Think about it, Howie — animation is so last century. Anthropomorphic filmmaking iswhere it's at. I can make more Fries and run my own studio."

"Wow!"

"Yep." He patted Howie on the shoulder. "And don't worry, I won't forget any of my friends."

"But I'm your *only* friend. And remember, you promised me the Pâté du Pooty cheese hunk from Paris."

After school Freddy and Howie were in for a shock. The Fries were gone.

"Omigosh, what could have happened to them?" Freddy said frantically as he looked everywhere inside the barn.

Howie pointed toward the woods, where there was a ragged gap in some bushes. "Looks like something went through there."

Just as they started running to the woods, a voice shouted "AHA!"

They stopped dead and looked behind them.

There stood Nancy Funkhouser wearing a baseball catcher's chest plate and face mask and holding a long wooden sword in her right hand.

"Oh no!" groaned Freddy, "Not now, Nanny Boo-Boo."

"I've caught you red-handed, Freddy," she

proclaimed. "And your creepy little cheese cube–snorting sidekick."

"Hey, I'm not creepy," snapped Howie. "I'm just small and misunderstood."

"What do you want?" asked Freddy. "And make it fast. We're busy."

Nancy advanced on them, her sword held at the ready. "Oh, I'm sure you *are* busy, you little fiend! And I know all about it."

"All about what?"

"You know perfectly well what, mister. Big, purple, and ugly."

"But your hair's red, Nanny Boo-Boo, not purple."

"Ha-ha," laughed Howie. "Good one, Freddy."

"Put a cork in it, you munchkin, before I use you for a shish-kabob." She pointed her sword menacingly at Howie, who fell backward, cowering. "Wait until I tell Dad what I saw, Freddy."

Freddy looked at her smugly. "Who cares? Tell dad anything you want. I'll be famous and rich and you won't." Freddy grabbed Howie, and they took off running to the woods.

A stunned Nancy looked after them. "Victory still shall be mine," she proclaimed, and then swung her sword up, accidentally conked her head, and knocked herself out.

CHAPTER 7

CURLY RUNS THE BASES

The Fries had run a long way through the woods and then stopped for a rest. When they finally started walking again, they came to a point where the trail branched off in three separate directions.

"Okay," began Theodore, "Wally, you and Ziggy go that way." He pointed to the right. "Curly, you and Si and Meese go that way." He pointed to his left. "And I'll head straight. If anyone finds a place where we all can hide, come and get the others."

"That is, like, a fabulous idea, Theodore," said Wally. "Why, if you keep coming up with stuff like that, you'll almost be as smart as me."

"I doubt I will ever attain your relatively unpretentious level of intellectual ability, Wally," replied Theodore.

Wally slapped Theodore on the back, almost knocking off his glasses. "Ahh, blue guy, you just never know."

Ten minutes later Freddy and Howie reached the spot where the trail branched off. "Okay, Howie," said Freddy, "you go to the left, and I'll go to the right. Then we'll meet back here and if we haven't found them we'll both go down the center trail."

The boys sprinted off in separate directions.

After they had walked a while, Si, Meese, and Curly came to a clearing where there was a road. They headed down the road for a bit until they heard some sounds coming from up ahead.

Si said, "I bet that right up ahead is the greatest thing in the whole world, and it's just waiting for us."

"I think we should go crawl under a rock," said Meese. "It's no more than we deserve."

"Why are you so negative all the time? Geez, it could start to get a Fry down, even a happy one like me," replied Si.

"I'm not negative," said Meese huffily, "I just know nothing but absolute destruction is waiting around the corner for me. So why deny it?"

"Five bucks says that right up there is something incredibly fun," challenged Si.

"You don't have five dollars. You don't even have *pockets*," Meese shot back.

Si bent down and picked something up. He showed them a five dollar bill. "Lucky is as lucky does. Okay, put your money where your pout is. Five bucks."

"I don't have any money," wailed Meese. "And besides, I'd just lose."

"Okay, I'll bet you a buck and I'll lend you the money."

"Well, okay, but I'm sure this is going to be a total disaster."

"Just be prepared to pay up when you lose." He glanced over at Curly, who had stretched up high and was looking for the source of the sounds they were hearing.

"Right, Curly?" asked Si.

"Idon'tknow,Ihopeso,becauseIdon'twanttoget-intotrouble," mumbled Curly.

"See, even Curly agrees with me," proclaimed Si happily. "Let's go."

They rounded the bend in the road. Off to the left was a baseball field. Two teams were playing and a bunch of people were in the stands watching and cheering.

"Oh, goody," said Si. "A game. See, I told you. What fun. Come on!"

"ButFreddysaidnottoletanyoneseeus," mumbled Curly.

"See, Curly wants to have fun too," said Si. He dragged Meese along, and Curly reluctantly followed.

Right about the time they got to the field, the batter hit a long fly ball over the left field fence.

Without thinking, Curly uncoiled, went up twenty feet in the air, and caught the ball. He looked apprehensively at Si and Meese.

"Great catch, Curly," shouted Si. "Here, throw me the ball."

Curly tossed it to him. Si climbed the fence and waved the ball in the air, bopping Meese in the nose with the ball twice.

"Give me that!" shouted Meese angrily, and he made a grab for the ball.

"Hey, okay, let's play takeaway," said Si gleefully.

"We're attached to each other, you moron," shot back Meese. "Even if *I* take it away, *you'll* still have it."

"Uhguysyoubetterlookwhat'shappening'cause-Idon'tthinkit'stoogood," mumbled Curly frantically.

"What was that, Curly?" asked Si.

"We'reinbigtrouble!" Curly mumbled, and he pointed at something.

Si and Meese stopped fighting over the ball and looked where Curly was pointing. All the baseball players and all the people in the stands were running at them, and they didn't look very happy. In fact, they looked like they might do the Fries bodily harm if they could just get to them.

Meese did the only thing he could think of. He started to bawl.

"No time for crying. Happy foot, don't fail me now," yelped Si as he tossed the ball to Curly and took off running, pulling Meese along.

Curly caught the ball and started to run after Si and Meese. But then he saw another person running at him. He didn't recognize that it was Howie. He uncoiled to his full height, turned, and ran past all the people coming at him.

Astonished, the crowd turned and chased him. Curly ran around the bases and the crowd followed. But he was so fast that he kept passing them. But he did so politely and always said, "Excusemepardonmecomingthroughthanks," and tipped his ball cap to the ladies.

Finally the people finally ran out of breath and stopped. Curly turned to face the crowd.

"Give me the ball," said one of the ballplayers.

"Yeah, throw it here," called out another player.

"No, give it to me," shouted a kid in the crowd.

Confused, Curly threw the ball way, way up in the air. When it came back down it was headed right for the crowd.

"I've got it!" yelled one ballplayer.

But another cried out, "No, I've got it!"

Then another and another and another screamed, "No, I've got the ball!"

All of the ballplayers collided with each other and collapsed in a big pile. Then the fans started after the ball and smacked into each other. By the time the ball landed, there was no one left standing to catch it.

Meanwhile, Howie had reached Curly, grabbed him by the hand, and they both disappeared into the woods. When the crowd untangled themselves, they were just left scratching their heads, wondering if they all had really just seen what they thought they had.

Back in the woods, Howie, Si, Meese, and Curly caught their breath.

"So what happened back there, Curly?" asked Howie.

Motioning with his hands, Curly mumbled, "Iranaroundincirclesuntiltheygottiredandthen."

He drew in a breath, and continued, "Ithrewthe-ballandtheyalltriedtocatchitand," he took another breath,"theyallfelldownandandIranawayand-hereIam."

"That's what I like about you, Curly, you're a Fry of few words," said Si.

Meese reached over and grabbed the five dollars out of Si's hand.

"What are you doing?" cried Si.

"I won the bet."

"But it was only for a dollar."

"We almost got killed. That's worth at least five bucks."

"But that was a lot of fun back there! You can't tell me you didn't enjoy that."

"Oh, shut up, mister happy foot!" snapped Meese.

"Come on, guys," interrupted Howie, "we need to find Freddy!"

CHAPTER 8

TOO MANY PIES

As Wally and Ziggy headed down the trail, Wally stopped and sniffed the air.

"Blueberries," he said after a long whiff. "And strawberries. And now I smell raspberries, and blackberries, and pumpkin, and apple and —"

Ziggy interrupted. "Look up there." Situated in a big field was a large brick building with twin chimneys out of which smoke was pouring.

"It's the Pookesville Pie Factory," observed Ziggy, pointing at the sign over the door.

Wally almost fainted. "Pies! That's my *favorite* finger food. Come on, Ziggy."

"Wait a minute. We came into the woods to hide. Freddy said not to let anyone see us. We can't go in there."

"Not to worry, little papoosie, it's, uh, lunch-time, so everybody will be out eating."

"How do you know that?"

"It's a food thing — you'll just have to trust me. Come on."

Wally put Ziggy on his broad shoulders and

sped toward the building. They slipped in the back door and looked around. Wally's big eyes grew even larger. The room was as large as a football field. There were big ovens at one end and lots of tables set up on the floor. And on each table there were dozens of different pies.

"Quick, Ziggy, pinch me, I must be dreaming," said Wally. Ziggy did as he was told. "Ouch," yelped Wally. "See, I told you, nobody here. All right, little Fry guy, you wait here while old Wally scouts out the place."

"Remember, Wally, those pies don't belong to us, so don't eat them."

"Eat them! Ziggy, what kind of Fry do you think I am?"

"A big, hungry one."

"Oh, I smell gooseberry."

Ziggy hid in the corner while Wally sneaked — to the extent that a large purple Fry can actually sneak anywhere — up to one of the tables and took a long sniff.

"Pumpkin," he said in a long, hungry moan. "My ninth favorite pie of all time. I could eat it all day." He started to stick his plump finger in one of the pies when he saw Ziggy staring at him.

"No, Wally. Be strong," cautioned the yellow Fry.

"If only I weren't so weak from hunger," he moaned.

He went farther down the row of tables so

that Ziggy couldn't see him.

"Getting weak ... resistance falling ... feel food frenzy coming on," Wally said in halting words. He picked up one of the pies and held it under his nose.

"Wally!" scolded Ziggy, who had followed him.

"Aw, come on, Zig. They have so many pies. They won't even miss it."

Ziggy thought about it. "Well, okay, I guess. But only *one* bite."

"Oh, thank you, thank you, thank you!" Wally looked around. "But which one? Apple ...? Or blueberry ...? Pumpkin ...? Or banana cream over there ...? And there's strawberry. Yum, I love strawberry. Oh, there's Key lime over there. Me LOVE Key lime. I want them all. Can't decide, mind failing, resistance nearly gone, must try and stop ... but ..."

As he was talking Wally's eyes started spinning and his tongue started wagging like a big, thirsty dog. His fingers were bending and unbending and his belly was heaving up and down.

"Uh, Wally, are you okay?" asked Ziggy.

Right at that moment, Freddy ran panting into the pie factory and saw Wally and Ziggy.

"Just fine, little papoosie. Wally's just ... just ... just ... FFFFFFIIIINNNNEEEE!"

"No!" yelled Freddy. "Don't!"

Ziggy saw it coming too and ducked just in time. Wally opened his mouth as wide as he could and took one humongous breath. All of sudden there was an enormous suction force in the room. The tables started to quiver and the windows rattled and the tablecloths started whipping around.

Then the first pie flew off the table and was sucked right into Wally's gaping mouth. Another pie — a key lime — zipped right through the air, followed by several others. Then the whole table of key limes followed. And then the apples, and banana creams, and raspberries... and within barely a minute every pie in the place was now in Wally's bulging mouth. The purple Fry was now so large that his belly touched one wall and his butt the other.

Hearing the commotion, the pie factory workers ran out of another room and were immediately caught in the suction. They grabbed onto pipes that ran along the wall so they wouldn't end up in Wally's mouth too. When Wally finally closed his mouth and gave a huge swallow, the suction stopped and the workers fell to the floor.

Ziggy stared at his purple friend with his huge eyes. "Wally, look what you did. I said just one bite!"

"Well, it *was* only one bite. There was just a lot in it."

"Hey, you!" shouted one of the workers, pointing at Wally and Ziggy.

"Wally, Ziggy!" yelled Freddy. "Run, guys!" He ducked down before the man saw him.

"Oh boy, time to head out, little papoosie," said Wally.

"But we have to stay here and explain all this," countered Ziggy. "I'm sure they'll understand."

Wally stared at the men as they picked up chairs and sticks and came at them like junkyard dogs circling an intruder.

"We'll write 'em a letter instead," hissed Freddy. "Come on!"

But now they were surrounded. As Wally shrank back, one of the workers came forward holding a stick.

"Okay, what's your name?" the worker called out to Ziggy.

Ziggy's little face scrunched up into something very frightening.

"MY NAME IS ZIGGY!" he screamed so loudly

that the force of air coming out of his mouth knocked the stick out of the man's hand. But in his excitement Ziggy bumped his head against a table and his arms, legs, and face immediately fell off.

All the workers screamed at this horrible sight and fled the room.

Wally looked at most of Ziggy lying on the floor. "Wow, little papoosie, that was really cool. How'd you do that?"

Ziggy's mouth moved from where it was on the floor. "I don't know. And how do I put myself back together?"

Freddy ran up, kicked Ziggy in the butt, and all his parts sprang back up and reattached themselves.

"Sorry, Ziggy, I didn't have time to tell you about that special feature of yours. I thought, you know, it would be kind of funny."

"Hey, how'd you do that?" asked Wally.

"Relative theory of magnetic conductivity and reverse polarity phenomenon."

"That would've been my guess," concluded Wally.

Freddy said, "Now let's get out of here before they come back."

They ran out as fast as they could go, which wasn't all that fast since Wally was so much bigger now.

Once outside they hurried into the woods, but Wally slowed down and then stopped. He let out a burp so loud that five squirrels fell out of a tree and three deer roaming nearby fainted from sheer terror. "Not feeling too good," complained Wally.

"Well, I guess so. You just ate four hundred pies!" exclaimed Ziggy.

"Four hundred? You sure? Seemed closer to two-fifty. OOOOHHHH! Be right back," mumbled Wally. He ran behind some trees. Freddy and Ziggy heard a bunch of disgusting sounds, and when Wally came back he was normal size — at least for a huge purple thing.

"Feel better?" asked Freddy.

"Lots," he said with a big smile and rubbed his hands together. "So, we had dessert. What say we grab a little lunch?"

Freddy could only stare at the big purple guy. Then he walked off, shaking his head while Ziggy followed him, doing the very same thing.

They came back to where the trails branched off and found Howie, Curly, and Si and Meese waiting for them there.

"Where's Theodore?" asked a frantic Freddy.

Curly pointed down the center path. "Hewentthataway."

Freddy paled. "But that leads to downtown Pookesville!"

"Oh boy!" exclaimed Howie. "That isn't good."

"All of you just stay here," yelled Freddy, and he ran as fast as he could toward downtown Pookesville.

CHAPTER 9

THE POOKESVILLE CHESS MATCH

Theodore had walked until he reached the downtown area of Pookesville. Keeping out of sight as Freddy had instructed, he arrived in the very center of town. Here there was a park with a brick courtyard, a few bushes and trees, and a statue of Captain Peter Pookes. The captain was a Civil War veteran who had founded the town when he got lost from his regiment, wandered around, built a shack, and then refused to leave, as founders of towns often do. There were about four hundred pigeons currently sitting on his statue. Pigeons loved Captain Pookes.

Two very old men were sitting on a park bench playing chess next to Captain Pookes. Theodore loved chess, and forgetting Freddy's warning to remain hidden, he walked over. Theodore stared over the old men's stooped shoulders and quickly sized up the match.

He said, "Let me see, rook to F-five would be the most advantageous, I believe."

Neither of the old men even bothered to look

up. One of them grumbled, "There's a chess master in every crowd." Both men cackled. But Theodore did note that the old guy playing with the black pieces made that very move.

The old guy playing with the white pieces laughed and said, "That'll cost you, Jasper. You made a big blunder there, you old coot." He moved his white bishop forward.

"All right, Jasper," said Theodore, studying the board, "Now, knight to D-three, and we have discovered check."

"Heh-heh, Charlie," said Jasper, "Looks like I'm gonna kick your skinny little hiney-butt this time."

"This can't be!" cried out Charlie as he stared at the board. Neither of them had even looked at Theodore. "There's gotta be a way out."

"Unfortunately, there isn't," said Theodore. "I would surrender with all due haste and humility."

Charlie kept staring at the board, looking for an escape. Finally, realizing the situation was hopeless, he slowly laid down his king in a show of defeat.

"Yee-ha!" shouted Jasper. "Checkmate, you old coot, you. First time in thirty years. All right, pay up, fifty cents, right in my hot little hand."

Charlie pulled out the coins and gave them to Jasper. "Okay, but next time, put *him* in check, all right?" Charlie looked up at Theodore and froze. "ALIEN!" he screamed.

Theodore looked around with alarm. "Alien? Where?"

"There!" Charlie said, pointing right at him. Jasper looked at Theodore and started yelling too. "Help! Police!"

"Help! Police!" cried Theodore. "Aliens, there are aliens!"

Charlie and Jasper got up and ran — rather, they hobbled briskly — with their canes down the sidewalk, away from Theodore.

People were hustling out of their stores and houses to see what the fuss was. The minister came tearing out of the church.

"What's going on?" he yelled. "We're trying to have a wedding rehearsal."

Theodore came running up behind him. "Aliens. It's aliens! Get the police."

"Aliens?" said the minister skeptically. "Where?" He turned and saw Theodore.

"AAAAHHHH!" screamed the minister.

"Do you see them?" Theodore asked urgently.

The minister backed up, pointing at Theodore and trying to say something, but he couldn't quite get it out. By now everyone in town was pouring into the streets. When they spotted Theodore they all started shouting, and picking up things to throw at him.

It finally dawned on the blue Fry. "They think *I'm* the alien. Quite ridiculous." He faced the growing crowd. "Listen, all of you, I'm not an alien."

They stared at back at him, unconvinced.

"Now I know that I look different than all of you, but I'm also quite intelligent, kind, and well-mannered. I'm sure that we'll all get along wonderfully."

There was silence and then a man shouted, "I say we squash the big blue thing!"

"YEAH! SQUASH HIM!" yelled the crowd in unison.

"Oh dear," said Theodore. "I do believe they intend me harm." He took a step back, and then another and another. "You know, you really should treat visitors to your town with a little more courtesy." When the crowd started coming at him carrying big sticks, he used his enormous brain to come up with a stellar plan.

He turned and ran as fast as he could.

"Alien!" screamed the crowd as they ran after him.

"Barbarians!" yelled a terrified Theodore.

He increased his pace, turned a corner, and ducked down another street.

"Theodore!"

Theodore looked ahead of him.

It was Freddy. He was standing at the end of the street and waving at him. "This way, quick!"

Theodore shot ahead, joined Freddy, and they turned the corner and ran hard.

"How are we going to get away?"

"Just follow me; I'll think of something." Freddy ducked down another street and Theodore followed.

As he was running down the street, Freddy eyed a store with an awning out front. Behind the store was a railroad track down which a train was slowly moving. "All right — angle of trajectory, speed of us, speed of train, mass times energy, gravitational factors, friction pattern, wind velocity and direction," Freddy said to himself. "Theodore, listen carefully, here's the plan." Freddy told him his idea. "Your timing has to be perfect."

"As a genius I will accept nothing less of myself. But you're sure I can do it?"

"I built your legs with a core of coiled aluminum. It's the same material that lets Curly rise up in the air."

A minute later the crowd turned the corner and saw Theodore. The same man yelled, "Squash him!"

"I bet he was a nasty little child, too," said Theodore. What the crowd couldn't see was that Freddy was curled up in a little ball against Theodore's chest, holding tightly onto the blue Fry.

"YEEEEE-HAAAAAA!" yelled Theodore as he leaped high up into the air, hit the awning,

bounced on it like a trampoline, shot to the sky, stretched as far as he could, and snagged the last car on the train with the tip of his left pinky. He pulled himself up onto the train while Freddy ducked down so the crowd couldn't see him. Theodore adjusted his glasses and tidied his bowtie. He looked down at the crowd.

"Well," he called out, "what did you expect from a genius? Hasta la vista, baby!"

The man in the crowd who had wanted to squash Theodore looked at the person next to him.

"Hey, he's pretty smart for a big blue thing."

"Yeee-haaa?" said Freddy as the train rolled away from Pookesville.

Theodore looked embarrassed. "Despite my scholarly demeanor, I've always harbored a secret ambition to be a cowboy."

Freddy lay down on top of the train and closed his eyes. "A blue cowboy."

"What did you say, Freddy?"

"Oh, nothing."

The train rolled on.

CHAPTER 10

ALL FALL DOWN

Freddy and Theodore hooked up with all the others and headed back to Freddy's laboratory to hide after Freddy convinced them it would be safe. The Fries had told him about his sister discovering them. "I'll take care of that," he said.

On the way back the Fries shared their adventures with one another.

"Those people wouldn't even listen to me," said Theodore indignantly as he brushed dirt and grime off his bowtie. "It was most undignified having to escape on the top of a train, of all things."

"Well, what about us?" wailed Meese. "We were almost trampled to death by people who throw little balls around and then cheer about it."

"Yeah, it was the coolest thing that ever happened to me," said Si excitedly. Meese bopped him on the head.

"Wow, nice punch there, Meese," noted Si. "You're a good hitter."

Howie said, "I've never been to a baseball

game like that. Pretty weird."

"Well, I had a great time at the pie factory," said Wally.

"He threw up all over the forest," said Freddy. "It was pretty disgusting. All the animals gave us really mean looks for destroying their home."

Wally replied in an offended tone, "Hey, I offered to clean it up."

"Yeah, using a leaf," shot back Ziggy.

"One of the squirrels bit me in the butt. I think it left a mark," complained Wally.

When they got to Freddy's lab, the Fries looked around in amazement at all the equipment and gadgets.

"Cool, little dudee-rudee," commented Wally. "So can you, like, invent food with all this stuff?"

Theodore pointed to a wall of odd-looking things. "What are those?"

"Things my dad invented. Anti-gravity flight belts, pill slingers, neuromuscular disruptors, you know, just your basic stuff." Freddy looked at all the Fries. "Okay, guys," he said, "After what happened today, you've *really* got to stay here in my lab. Okay?"

The Fries all nodded.

"Let's go, Howie," said Freddy.

When they reached the farmhouse, they stopped dead. There was a police car in the driveway. And there was Adam Spanker's father, Police Chief Stewie Spanker, confronting Alfred Funkhouser.

Behind them, on their motor scooters, were Adam Spanker and his gang, looking very, very happy.

"Wow, cool," said Howie. "Is your dad going to be, like, arrested? I've never seen anybody arrested before except on TV."

"No, he's not going to be arrested," answered Freddy hotly. He stared nervously at the police chief and the Spanker gang. "At least I hope he's not." He paused and added, "I wonder what Dad's blown up now?"

Freddy and Howie ran up to Alfred, who was holding something that looked like twenty pairs of scissors connected together and attached to a large battery thingamajig in his right hand. He held a large pizza pie in his left hand.

"Dad, what's going on?" asked Freddy.

"I'm not sure what's going on, actually. Chief Spanker wanted to talk to me."

Chief Stewie Spanker looked just like his son except bigger and meaner. "Look, Funkhouser," said Chief Spanker, getting right in Alfred's face, "we know you like to do crazy experiments and come up with stupid gadgets."

"Stupid gadgets?" exclaimed Alfred. "I don't invent stupid gadgets."

"He invents *useful* stuff," said Freddy defensively. "Like . . . well, like the . . ."

"Like the tomato-seed shooters," prompted his father.

"Right," said Freddy, "and the salad that comes up out of the ground all ready to be tossed in a bowl. Dad gave that formula away to everyone in Pookesville for free."

"Yeah, well, that salad had a certain odor to it," growled Chief Spanker.

"That's what they invented air fresheners for," advised Alfred.

Freddy added excitedly, "And then there's the non-nuclear mosquito defeater. And the anti-gravity flight belt."

"Still working out some control problems on that one," pointed out his father.

"And then there's the neuromuscular disruptor to capture criminals."

"The Jelly Legger, I like to call it," said Alfred proudly. "You should get some for the police department, Chief."

"And then there's the burp pill for upset stomachs," added Freddy.

Chief Spanker looked very upset. "I actually tried that one. Everything came out the other end . . . for days!"

"That's why I renamed it the pooper pill," said Alfred.

Chief Spanker stared pointedly at the scissor thing. "So what's that, a new gadget to cut hair?"

"Oh, this?" said Alfred. "It's a battery-powered pizza cutter that cuts an entire pizza into perfect slices in two seconds. Here, I'll show you."

He handed the pizza to Spanker, turned on the battery, and engaged the scissors. Two seconds later the pizza remained uncut, but the police chief had no hat left — and no hair, either.

"Oh dear," said Alfred, staring at the now nearly bald policeman. "I thought I had worked that problem out. Well, actually, it *does* have application for hair cutting. If you come into the Burger Castle I'll give you some of our fat-free fries. They're good at growing hair back."

Spanker snatched the scissors contraption out of Alfred's hands and threw it down. "I wouldn't be caught dead in that dumpy restaurant of yours. And assaulting a police officer is a crime."

"But I didn't mean to —"

"Throw him in jail, Dad," shouted Adam. "And his nutcase son too."

"I wish you'd ask your son not to call my son names," said Alfred.

"Hey, hey!" yelled Chief Spanker, sticking a big finger in Alfred's chest. "You watch your mouth. Adam is a very sensitive boy."

"But I didn't —"

"Give it a rest, Funkhouser, you're in enough

trouble." The policeman consulted his notebook. "Now let me see, two months ago you attempted to launch a trash can into orbit using a rocket engine attached to the roof of your Dodge station wagon. Said trash can did not make it into orbit but rather came down and landed in the community swimming pool three miles away. Call me silly, but that seems a little crazy."

"Well, first of all, it wasn't a trash can," explained Alfred Funkhouser.

"That's right," said Freddy. "It was a solar-powered meteorological data-gathering platform designed to circle the ionosphere and transmit valuable information back to the home station."

"Well, when it landed in the swimming pool it looked just like a trash can," responded Spanker impatiently. "Now, let's get to today's events." He looked at his notebook again. "We have three separate incidents of large, colorful creatures causing considerable trouble in the area. First, a red thing with —" Spanker checked his notes again and shook his head, "— two heads and a green thing that rose way up in the air disrupted a local baseball game, causing considerable mayhem and a number of injuries."

The police chief continued. "Next, the Pookesville Pie Factory was attacked, and four hundred pies eaten by a fat purple thing that had a little yellow sidekick whose face, arms, and legs fell off. Lastly, a large blue thing that knew how to play chess really well created hysteria in downtown Pookesville and then escaped by jumping onto a moving train." The policeman closed his notebook and tapped it against Alfred's chest. "Now are you going to try and tell me that you had nothing to do with all that, Funkhouser?"

With each description, Freddy's eyes grew wider and wider and his stomach started doing bigger and bigger flip-flops. *This was all going so wrong.*

Alfred was staring at his son, his hand rubbing

his very sharp chin, a sure sign his brain was on high-speed computing mode. "A fat purple thing that could eat four hundred pies? A two-headed red thing and a yellow creature who loses body parts? A blue thing that could play chess and jump on moving trains, and a green thing that could rise way up in the air?"

"Yeah!" cried out Chief Spanker as he slapped his notebook against his beefy hand. "Now what do you say to that?"

"Well, I personally don't know anything about it. It would have taken quite a scientist to come up with something like that. In fact, I wish it had been me."

"Oh you do, do you? Well, we're going to give you some time to think about that. Come on, you're under arrest."

Spanker took out his handcuffs and put them on Alfred.

A cheer went up through the Spanker gang. "You tell him, Dad," yelled Adam.

"Wait, you can't arrest my dad," cried Freddy.

"Oh, I can't, can't I? Give me one good reason why not. He's the only one in town who makes crazy things like that. You Funkhousers have been trouble since the first day you came to Pookesville."

"You'll be an old man by the time you get out of jail, Funkhouser," taunted Adam.

A terrified Freddy stared at everyone. Adam shot him raspberries and raised his paintball gun menacingly. Chief Spanker eyed Freddy with disgust. But the worst thing of all was Freddy's father looking at him.

"But . . . but," stammered Freddy.

"What's the matter, Funky," said Adam, "C-c-ca-cat got your tongue?"

"It's okay, Freddy," said his father calmly. "I'll go downtown and get this all straightened out."

"Yeah, right," said Chief Spanker, belly laughing. "I'd get used to not having your father around for a while," he said as he led Alfred away.

"But we have to work on our float for the parade," protested Freddy.

Adam howled. "Wait'll you see the Patty Cakes float. You haven't got a chance, Funkhouser."

Chief Spanker put Alfred in the patrol car.

Freddy was trying hard not to cry in front of Adam and his gang, but he couldn't help himself. He ran to the police car and put his face against the window where his father was sitting.

"Dad —" he said tearfully.

"It's okay," his father said quietly. "I'll be home in time for supper. Go find your sister and tell her what happened."

The car drove off and Adam and his gang immediately circled around Freddy and Howie.

"Something tells me you two know a lot more

than you're saying, Funky," said Adam accusingly.

Freddy and Howie drew closer to each other. "You . . . you're tres . . . trespa—" Freddy stammered.

"Yeah, yeah, whatever." Adam looked through the open doors of the large barn that sat across from the farmhouse. "Hey, what do we have here?" He and his gang raced into the barn.

"Stop!" cried Freddy. He and Howie chased after them.

Inside the barn was the Funkhouser's float for the Founders' Day parade. Alfred had taken an old tractor chassis and put a flatbed trailer over it. The Funkhousers had built a wooden frame on top of the flatbed trailer in the form of a giant Vroom shake. Nancy also had added a platform at the top of the shake made to look like a balcony, where she could deliver her Shakespeare monologues to her adoring fans; it was accessed by a trapdoor in the platform.

Adam and his gang circled it. "This is the biggest piece of junk I've ever seen," said Adam, kicking one of the old tires and rattling the wooden frame.

"Hey, look at this," said one of his gang. He pointed to a banner that read: "The Burger Castle: the King of Groovy Food."

"What a pack of baloney," said Adam. He reached up and tore down the banner.

"Stop!" cried out Freddy.

Adam turned to him. "What did you say?"

Freddy turned pale. "I . . . I said, I mean . . ."

Howie confronted Adam. "He said stop it, you big fathead! Now get out before there's trouble."

Adam towered over Howie, who gulped and quickly stepped behind Freddy.

"I tell you what I'm gonna do, Funky. I'm gonna put this stupid float out of its misery." He turned to his gang. "Ready, boys?"

"Ready," they all answered.

"Charge," commanded Adam. He and his gang attacked the float and within minutes turned it into a big pile of junk. Then Adam grabbed Freddy and threw him on top of the pile of junk.

"See ya, Funky," laughed Adam. He and his gang got on their motor scooters and rode off.

"Freddy," said Howie fearfully, "are you okay?"

Freddy lay sprawled on top of the ruined float. "Actually, Howie, I'm getting used to this."

At that moment Nancy came into the barn and shrieked when she saw what had happened to the float. "Freddy Funkhouser, what have you done?"

Freddy lifted his head and started to explain. "It wasn't my . . . oh, forget it."

"Ruined. Absolutely ruined. It's over, all over. We can't possibly fix this in time," she said tearfully. "I'm going to tell Dad. Where is he?"

"Uh, in jail," answered Howie meekly.

"Jail!"

"It's a long story, Nanny Boo-boo," said Freddy wearily.

"I'll get even with you if it's the last thing I do, Freddy," said his sister as she stalked out.

Howie said, "I guess I better be getting home."

"I guess so."

"Is there anything I can do?"

"Know a good lawyer?"

"Uh, no."

"How about a good psychiatrist?"

"Uh, no."

"Then there's nothing you can do."

After Howie left, Freddy just lay there. "Well," he said to himself, "at least there's one good thing. I don't see how it could possibly get any worse."

Unfortunately, Freddy could not have been any more wrong about that.

CHAPTER 11

QUEEN NANCY THE NICEST
OF NANTUCKET

Alfred returned to the farm later that day. Freddy and his sister gave him big hugs.

"Was it awful in jail, Dad?" asked Nancy.

"I was never in jail, dear," said her father.

"But Chief Spanker —" began Freddy.

"Wiser and calmer heads prevailed," said his father. "When I pointed out there was not a shred of evidence tying me to any of these claims of mischievous monsters, Judge Thackery immediately let me go. At least the Judge is no friend of the Spankers. But we're not out of the woods yet. Chief Spanker said he's going to keep a close eye on all of us. And there're a lot of angry people out there because of what happened. There's even been a big reward offered for their capture."

"Mischievous monsters?" said Nancy. "What are you talking about?"

Alfred looked at Freddy. "Didn't you tell

your sister what happened?"

"Uh, I kind of forgot."

Alfred quickly told Nancy all about it. Before he was even finished she was staring pointedly at her little brother. Under her breath she muttered, "Big purple thing, huh?"

Their father said, "Well, we've got to get going. We're going to be late for the dinner hour at the Burger Castle."

"But we never have any customers!" she declared.

"Now, dear. We still have to go. Some hungry person might come in by accident. I'll make dinner and you two go and wash up."

After Freddy ate dinner, he ran to his room to get his chicken costume before they headed to the Burger Castle. He stopped abruptly at his bedroom door. Taped on it was a drawing of Wally. And below the picture were the words "I know everything." And it was signed "You know who."

Freddy ripped down the picture and slowly trudged to his sister's room and knocked on the door.

"Enter, O guilty and shameful one!" his sister cried out.

Freddy went inside. His sister was sitting on the bed wearing a long green cape with a big, high collar and a red paper crown. She held a scepter that was really her baton, and wore large brown boots on her feet. She looked like a giant grasshopper with red hair. Her big costume trunk stood open next to her bed.

Freddy stared at her. "Uh, Nanny Boo-Boo, what are you doing?"

"Ah, my loyal subject. Down on your knees before your queen."

Freddy's eyes bugged out. "*Excuse* me?"

His sister rose. "Or I'll just have to go and tell Dad all about what I saw outside your deeesssgggust-ing lab today."

"I don't know what you're talking about."

"A big purple blob called Wally?"

"Doesn't ring a bell."

"Let me refresh your memory. The same big purple thing ate four hundred pies at a pie fac-tory. And then there was a big blue thing that scared the town of Pookesville to death. And a green and a red thing with two heads that put an entire baseball team in the hospital."

"It was only the emergency room."

"Aha!" cried out Nancy triumphantly. "I knew it. At first you didn't care who knew. You were going to be rich and famous, but now you can't let anyone find out, can you? Well, it's going to cost you, you little brainiac." She peered down at him smiling evilly. "Here's the deal. You'll do exactly as I say from now on."

"Aw, stick a cheese cube up your nose."

Nancy went to the door and called down the hallway. "Oh, Dad . . . Freddy can explain why the police were here today."

"Hold on, hold on!" said Freddy frantically as he shut the door. If Chief Spanker found out about this he would never believe that it was just Freddy's doing. He would think Freddy's dad was involved and his father would go to jail for real. But even more than that, Freddy didn't want his dad to find out that he'd made the Fries in the first place. He'd used his father's super secret potatoes and nanotechnology without permission. Worse, he'd created the Fries without thinking through the consequences, like his father had taught him to.

His sister was waiting expectantly. Finally, Freddy answered reluctantly, "Okay."

"Now, my list of demands," said his sister as she unfolded a piece of paper that was so long it went all the way to the floor. "First, from now on, no more Nanny Boo-Boo. Now my name is Queen Nancy the Nicest of Nantucket."

Freddy stared at her dumbly. "We've never even been to Nantucket," he said, "and you're not really very nice."

"I know that! I just like the way it sounds. Next, you'll do all my chores and give me all your allowance."

"But —" Freddy began to protest, but she cut him off.

"Next," she went on, "When it's my turn to take out the trash you'll do it for me."

"But that's not fair!"

"Oh, Father," she called out, "do you want to hear about a big, fat purple —"

Freddy clamped his hands around her mouth. "Okay, okay, I'll take out the trash."

"Next, you'll make my breakfast, carry my books to school, help me with my science home-work, and . . ." The list just went on and on. And poor Freddy just knelt there on one knee and agreed to it all. What else could he do?

"Is that all, Nanny B —" he finally said.

"Tut, tut, tut, remember what we discussed."

"Yeah, well, I'm —"

"Oh, Father," she shouted, "I have something important to tell you."

"Okay, okay," said Freddy quickly. He sighed. "Queen Nancy the Nicest."

"Of Nantucket," she added.

"Of Nantucket," Freddy grumbled.

CHAPTER 12

THE CALM BEFORE THE STORM

After the Funkhousers got back from the Burger Castle that night, Freddy raced to his lab to see the Fries.

Wally wailed, "Look, little dudiski, I haven't eaten in over four hours! I'm starving to death." He tapped Theodore on the shoulder. "Look at me, Theodore. Can you still see me or am I too thin?"

Theodore took off his glasses and wiped them. "I don't need my glasses to see you, Wally. In Latin you would be known as *purpulis enormosis.*"

"*Purpulis enormosis,*" Wally bellowed. "That sounds important."

"So is everything okay?" asked Ziggy. "Are we still going to be famous?"

"I don't even know if I've figured out a way for us to keep on living in this country," answered Freddy despondently.

"Is it really that bad?" asked Theodore.

"The police arrested my dad, property was

damaged, people went to the hospital, and the whole town is up in arms," said Freddy. "Other than that, everything's great."

"Is there anything we can do to help?" squeaked Ziggy.

"Not that I can think of, Ziggy, but thanks for asking."

"Whew, that's a relief," said Wally. "Okay, let's eat."

"I'll get some food and bring it down to you," said Freddy. "Is there anything else you guys need?"

"Well, some books would be nice," answered Theodore. "Some good literature."

"All right!" exclaimed Wally. "I love good literature." He paused and added, "That's a cheese, right?"

"That's *limburger*!" said Theodore in exasperation.

Si piped in, "Well, you could bring some cards back. That way I can play Meese and get my five bucks back."

"Well, of course you will. I always lose!" complained Meese.

"Do you want anything, Ziggy?" asked Freddy.

The little Fry thought for a moment. "Well, do you have a spare blanket?"

"Sure thing," said Freddy kindly. "Okay, books, cards, blanket." He looked over at where Curly was keeping watch by the window. "Curly, do you want anything?"

Curly mumbled, "CouldIpleasehaveaball-andglove?"

"You bet, Curly, I have those in my room. I'll throw some with you."

Curly blew his nose and wiggled his ears in thanks.

Just then, Freddy's special phone rang. Someone was at the entrance to the lab.

Freddy answered it, "Who's there?"

"Howie Kapowie."

"Password?"

"Adam Spanker poops in his pants."

Freddy pressed a button, there was a scream, and Howie fell from the ceiling and into a pile of straw.

"I thought you were going to fix that," complained Howie. "Now I've got hay up my butt."

"I've been a little *busy*, Howie," Freddy shot back.

"I came here to tell you something really important. I was at my aunt's flower shop today when this stranger came in and ordered a bunch of flowers to be delivered to the Spankers' restaurant the day before the parade. I saw his car outside. It had New York license plates."

"Was he well-dressed and short with blond hair and a thin mustache?"

"That's him."

"Like you said I bet he's some big-shot

designer they hired to build their float for them. That means the Spankers *are* breaking the rules."

"I bet they are, but there's no way for us to prove it."

"I guess that's true," sighed Freddy.

Howie pulled out a cheese cube and was about to pop it in his mouth when a long purple arm shot out and snagged it.

"Hey," cried out Howie as he watched his cheese cube disappear into the abyss of Wally's mouth.

"MMMM. Me love cheese cubes," said Wally. "Do you have any more?" He headed toward Howie, who started backing up.

"Uh, Freddy, I'm getting ready to pee in my pants here," yelled a terrified Howie.

"More cheese cubes," said Wally, as though in a trance as he stalked toward Howie. "Need cheese cubes, feeling faint . . . need cheese." He lifted Howie off the ground, turned him upside down, and shook the little boy until a bunch of cheese cubes fell out of Howie's pockets. Wally sucked these up in an instant. Then he pulled on Howie's shirt. "Is this edible?"

"FREDDY!" screamed Howie. "I'm about to be eaten over here, for crying out loud."

Freddy made Wally drop Howie. "Come on, Howie, you can go to the house with me and help me bring some supplies to the Fries."

A few minutes later Freddy and Howie slipped into the farmhouse. Freddy listened at the door of his father's bedroom.

"Okay, he's asleep," he whispered to Howie. "We'd better make sure my sister's asleep too."

When they got to Nancy's bedroom door they heard the most awful noise.

Howie covered his ears. "What is that? Sounds like an elephant farting."

"Just my sister snoring. Okay, let's get to work."

They piled food, books, balls and gloves, playing cards, a blanket, and other supplies into a wagon and quickly returned to the lab and handed them all out. Howie played ball with Curly while Theodore read and Ziggy lay down with his blanket. Freddy sat by himself in a corner and stared at a wall. One by one the Fries and Howie stopped what they were doing to watch him.

"You okay, Freddy?" asked Howie.

"You look very sad indeed," noted Theodore.

Freddy shook his head. "It's nothing. I'll be okay."

"I'll hit myself in the head and

make my arms, legs, and face fall off," offered Ziggy. The yellow Fry bopped himself in the head and flew apart. Freddy kicked Ziggy in the butt, and the Fry sprang back together.

"Thanks, Ziggy," said Freddy, but he still looked sad.

"I can bop Meese in the head and make him cry," suggested Si. "He likes to cry."

"I do," admitted Meese. "In fact the only time I'm happy is when I'm bawling my guts out."

"You know, Freddy, if friends can't ask other friends to help, there's something undoubtedly wrong with such a scenario," said Theodore.

Freddy thought about this for a minute. "Well, maybe there is something you can do."

Howie and all the Fries eagerly gathered around him.

"There's a Founders' Day parade in two days, and we were going to enter the float competition," began Freddy. Then he quickly told the Fries all about the Burger Castle, the Patty Cakes restaurant, and about Adam Spanker and his gang and what they had done to the Burger Castle float.

"And Spanker's family controls this town. His dad's the police chief who arrested my father and who's still looking to get him over what happened."

"It sounds like the first step is to refurbish as expeditiously as possible your entry in the competition," said Theodore.

"Yeah, but first we better fix that thingie-thing they want in the parade," said Wally.

Theodore looked at his purple friend in exasperation. "That's what I just *said.*"

"You guys really want to help me?" asked Freddy.

"You bet," they all yelled together.

"Okay, let's get going. Lead the way, Freddy," said Howie.

CHAPTER 13

FRENCH-FRIED MIRACLE

They all stood in the doorway of the barn and looked at the wrecked float.

"So that's what a float looks like, huh, Freddy?" asked Ziggy.

"It sure is a beauty," said Si as he stared at the mess.

Meese cocked his head and stared at it. "I don't know; it sort of looks how I feel all the time."

Theodore stated firmly, "Curly, you keep a lookout. Wally, you and Ziggy clear away all the ripped-up material. Si, Meese, and Howie can start assembling materials that we can use. Freddy and I will put together some conceptual plans for what the actual end result will resemble."

"Don't you think you better draw a picture of what you want it to look like first?" asked Wally.

"THAT'S WHAT HE JUST SAID!" yelled Ziggy so loud they all jumped. Wally actually grabbed onto the barn rafters in his fright.

"Ziggy, keep it down," said Freddy. "My dad might hear you. Or worse yet, my sister."

"Sorry, Freddy," said Ziggy in his normally tiny voice.

Wally dropped down from the rafters and said, "That's okay, little psycho dude."

"Okay, men — er, Fries — let's get to work," said Freddy.

Theodore and Freddy had drawn up blueprints on the wall of the barn, and the restoration of the float had begun. Freddy said, "I never liked the design my sister came up with anyway. We're going to build it right this time."

Wally had morphed himself into a lumber mill planing saw, and board after board of wood ran through Wally's mouth as the purple Fry shaped it into usable pieces, but eating a couple of them along the way.

"Quality control," he explained with a burp.

Acting as a crane, Curly lifted the boards up and into place on the float platform, where Ziggy, who showed a natural talent for hitting things, pounded nails into the boards so fast with his hammer hands they could barely keep him supplied with enough.

Si, Meese, and Howie sewed fabric together and made decorations to place on the float. Then they found some old cans of paint in one of the storage buildings. Wally swallowed it and then shot it back out of his mouth. In under twenty minutes the entire float was perfectly painted.

Theodore and Freddy had checked and rechecked the tractor engine, supports, and tires.

"Your father built a very impressive turbocharged, air-cooled, electronic-ignition motor configuration," said Theodore.

"Yeah, there's no one better with gas flow than my dad," said Freddy.

By early morning they all stepped back and looked at the float. It was far better than before. It was a thing of beauty, actually. It wasn't a giant Vroom shake anymore; it was a miniature version of the Burger Castle that was actually hollow inside. Every detail was there, from the pickle turrets to the drawbridge and a painted yogurt moat. And on either side of the Burger Castle name were small fry figures.

Freddy ran his admiring gaze over it and then turned to his friends. "You guys really saved my butt. I don't know how to thank you."

"Food would be good," answered Wally.

"That's what friends do, Freddy," said Theodore. "Help each other."

"Yeah," said Howie, and he slapped Freddy on the back.

"Oh, no!" Ziggy was pointing up to the ceiling.

They all looked up and saw Si and Meese floating there.

"How'd you get up there?" demanded Freddy.

When Si and Meese opened their mouths to answer, they fell to the floor of the barn.

All the others rushed over to them.

"What happened?" asked Howie.

Si explained, "We were seeing who could hold their breath the longest when we started floating up."

"Hmm," said Freddy. "Hold your breath again, guys."

They did so and after five seconds they started to float up again.

"Now let out your breaths," cried out Freddy.

When they did, Freddy smelled the air. "Helium!" he said. "I didn't put that in when I designed you, but you are hollow. I know! When the lightning hit you, it must've caused a chemical reaction that makes your breath turn into helium when you hold it for longer than a few seconds. That actually might come in handy someday."

"Cool, I can fly," said Si.

"But I'm afraid of heights," wailed Meese.

"Well," said Freddy, "I think we need to call it a night."

Howie hurried home while the Fries returned

to the lab and Freddy went to his house and dropped into bed, exhausted.

Several hours later Nancy got up, went downstairs where her father was making breakfast, and said, "Dad, I didn't want to have to tell you this."

"Yes, Nanny-B, er, Nancy?"

"Our float for the Founders' Day parade's been destroyed."

"What! I can't believe it."

"It's true, Dad. Freddy did it. He's snapped this time, he really has. It's sad, very sad. Come on, I'll show you."

They raced to the barn and Nancy triumphantly threw open the door. "See?"

Alfred stared for a long moment and then exclaimed, "This is the most beautiful thing I've ever seen."

Nancy hadn't looked yet. "I know, it's awful, isn't it? I'll be happy to accept his allowance while he's in solitary confinement . . . what!" Nancy looked at the float in disbelief. "But it's all changed. It's . . . it's the Burger Castle. Where's the Vroom shake? Where's the balcony where I'm going to deliver my Shakespeare monologues?"

Her father smiled. "You *are* quite the actress. You really did surprise me."

"Uh, that's right, Dad. You know how I love surprises. In fact, I'm going upstairs right now to surprise Freddy. I'm sure he'll love it too."

She stomped off to go find her brother and cream him.

After she left, Alfred saw the blueprints that Freddy and Theodore had drawn on the wall. He started rubbing his very sharp chin. "I wonder," he said.

CHAPTER 14

HOWIE KAPOWIE SPILLS THE BEANS

Howie Kapowie was walking home from the store later that day when he was ambushed by Adam Spanker and his gang. They dangled him upside down and stuffed grass in his nose. Adam balled his huge, lumpy fists in front of Howie's upside-down face. "Tell me what you saw at Funky's place, or else."

"Nothing, I swear," wailed Howie as he blew grass out of his nose.

Adam grabbed Howie by his shirt. "I know that goofball's involved with all the crazy stuff that's happened. And you know about it. Now talk!"

"I know nothing!" shouted Howie.

Adam rubbed his four chins and studied the situation. "If you don't talk I'll make you give me the answers to all the tests in school."

"I already do!" said Howie.

"Oh yeah. Hmmm. I know. I'll break your bike in half."

"I don't care!"

"You don't?"

"No, because I don't have a bike."

"I'll steal your cat then."

"I'm allergic to them."

"I'll take your dog."

"I'm allergic to slobber too."

"I'll smash your computer."

"I use my dad's."

"I'll break your glasses."

"My mom's an eye doctor. I get 'em by the dozen. And besides, I'm loyal to Freddy. Nothing you can threaten will break me." Howie started to laugh crazily. "You don't know who you're dealing with. A Kapowie never gives in. Never!"

One of Adam's bully friends whispered something to him. Adam started smiling. "Right. I'm glad I thought of that." He turned to Howie. "All right, if you don't talk, I'll make sure that you never, ever get another cheese cube to eat so long as you live."

"I'll tell you everything," said Howie Kapowie.

CHAPTER 15

THE ATTACK OF THE SPANKER GANG

Later that same night, after Freddy got home from working at the Burger Castle, he hustled to his lab to see the Fries. A storm had blown in and it had started to rain, so Freddy hurried along the path to the barn where his lab was hidden. Suddenly, something flew out of the dark and stung his arm.

"Yeow!" he yelled, and rubbed his arm, his fingers getting all sticky from something. "What the —"

"You're completely surrounded, Funkhouser," a voice boomed out. "Your butt is mine."

Freddy's spirits plummeted as he watched Adam Spanker and his gang rise up from behind a knoll, paintball guns in hand.

"What do you want?" Freddy called out fearfully.

"I want your freaky friends. I'm gonna turn 'em in and collect that big reward."

"You better get off my property before I call my dad."

Bam! Another paintball bullet hit him in the leg. It really hurt, but Freddy bit his lip and didn't cry out.

Adam laughed. "Like your dad scares me. He's as crazy as you."

"Don't you call my dad names!" said Freddy hotly.

Bam. Another shot in the other leg. Freddy felt like crying now, but he didn't. *Never, ever let the enemy see you cry*, he told himself.

"I'm waiting, Funky."

Freddy thought quickly. Suddenly he had a plan. It just might work, because Adam was like a T-rex — big body but little brain.

"Okay," Freddy said, "I give up. I can see there's no way out this time. But we have to go to my laboratory. It's over there." Freddy pointed to a large building down the path a bit. "Follow me."

"Okay, but no funny stuff. I'll be watching."

Freddy started walking toward one of the big barns as Spanker and his gang followed. When he got to the barn door, Freddy called out, "Okay, it's right in here."

"This better not be a trick, or you'll be really sorry," threatened Adam.

"It's not. You guys win. You're too tough for me." He went inside and the others followed.

"Okay, where are your freaky friends?" demanded Adam.

"They're hiding right over there," answered Freddy. He pointed at a large pen where a pig was laying in the muck. Freddy said, "I'll get them. They're kind of shy."

He went over, undid the latch on the gate to the pigpen, and suddenly smacked the pig on the rump. It squealed and took off running right at Adam and his gang. They all screamed and scattered as the big pig bore down on them.

While Adam and his gang were running away, Freddy grabbed a small wagon that was sitting next to the wall, pulled it through two loose boards at one end of the barn, and hurried over to a dirt path that ran to his laboratory. He pushed the wagon as fast as he could and then jumped on and flew down the dirt path.

Right about that time Adam and his gang burst out from the barn, shouting after him. Freddy felt paintball bullets whiz by his head. One of them hit his wagon. The rain was falling harder again, but Freddy didn't care. He heard Adam and his gang running after him, but he was going so fast they weren't gaining at all. He reached the barn, tripped the secret entrance, and fell through the trapdoor into his lab, landing in the pile of hay.

"Fries, it's me, Freddy."

All the Fries quickly assembled in front of him.

"What's wrong, Freddy?" asked Ziggy. "You look awful."

Freddy said, "Okay, here's the deal. Adam Spanker and his gang are heading this way and they're armed and dangerous. They've hit me three times, but nothing vital. When they attack, we'll pretend to fight them off and then we'll let them come inside. I've been working on some new inventions and modifying some of dad's old ones. So once Spanker and his gang get in here, we'll pulverize 'em."

"Wow, sounds like a lot of fun," said Si.

"We're all doomed," whined Meese. "And it'll all be your fault, Si."

"My fault! How could it be my fault?" asked Si.

"Because everything bad that happens to me is always your fault."

Freddy's phone rang. "Yeah?" he said.

"It's Howie."

"What's the password?"

"Adam Spanker sucks his thumb."

Freddy hit the button, and there was a scream as Howie landed in the pile of hay.

He jumped up quickly. "The Spanker gang tortured me and made me spill the beans on the Fries."

"I know, Howie. They're about to attack."

"I would've been here earlier but they tied me to a tree. I just got loose. Come on, we better get out of here."

"No, I'm going to stay and fight," declared Freddy.

"But we've always run from Adam Spanker, ever since kindergarten."

"I'm tired of running from him."

"But we've always thought that. So what's changed?" asked Howie.

Freddy looked at the Fries. "What's changed is we're not alone anymore, Howie. We have friends who'll fight right beside us. Won't you, guys?"

All the Fries stepped forward. "Let's kick some Spanker butt," yelled Wally.

"Okay, guys, listen up, here's the plan," Freddy said.

CHAPTER 16

FRIES VS. GUYS

When Adam and his gang reached the barn, he held up his hand for them to stop. He spoke into his walkie-talkie. "Have Big Benny ready just in case." He looked at his men. "Watch out for tricks," he warned.

They aimed their paintball guns and looked around. Suddenly they heard a sound, and something hit Adam in the arm. He reached down and picked it up. It was a pebble. He laughed. "This is all he has? We'll destroy 'em. Come on guys, charge!"

As they rushed forward a few more pebbles flew at them, but did no damage.

Adam laughed, "Funky, you are, like, so dead."

They reached the door to the barn, pulled it open, and raced inside. They looked around, their paintball guns pointing in all directions.

"All right, Funky, you better come out or else," shouted Adam.

Suddenly bright lights came on everywhere, and Freddy appeared at the top of the hayloft.

"Don't come any closer," he said in a quivering voice.

"Or what?" sneered Adam. "You gonna hit me with another pebble? Ohhh, owww, you're killing me. Please stop." The gang all laughed.

They all stopped laughing when they saw Freddy jump from the hayloft, but before he hit the ground he shot upward, right to the ceiling and hovered over them. Then Howie Kapowie came zooming out and hovered over them too. They both were wearing antigravity belts that Freddy's dad had invented that allowed them to fly.

"I'll give you five seconds to give up or else," said Freddy.

The gang looked up at them nervously but Adam sneered, "Or else what?"

Freddy held up his arm where the seed shooter was attached. Howie had one on too.

Adam belly-laughed. "Ooohh, you're gonna hit me with some tomato seeds; I can hardly stand the pain. Okay, guys, let's blow them out of the sky."

"Time's up," shouted Freddy. He looked at Howie and said, "Ready, aim, fire."

Freddy and Howie shot right at the gang. Tiny seeds shot out of the shooter, but as soon as they did, they swelled into something bigger. Far bigger.

"Owww!" yelled Adam as a pineapple hit him in the chest, knocking him on his butt.

"YOW!" cried another gang member next to him as an eggplant nailed him in the ear.

"Uggh!" said another bully as a fat pumpkin split open on his head.

The Spanker gang was being hit from all sides by a barrage of large fruit and vegetables as Howie and Freddy whizzed around the barn, shooting point blank.

"This is so much cooler than tomato seeds," yelled Howie as he hit Adam in the butt with a twelve-pound watermelon, sending him headfirst into a pile of old cow poop.

"It took me a couple of days to come up with the process to shrink all this stuff so it'd fit in the seed shooters, but it was sure worth it," said a smiling Freddy.

Within seconds the gang lay groaning on the floor of the barn. Freddy and Howie landed in front of them. Adam sat up and stared at them furiously. "You twerps are gonna pay for this. Come on, guys, charge!"

Adam and his gang rose up and sprinted toward Howie and Freddy. The two looked at each other and smiled. "Ready?" said Freddy.

"Ready, roger will-co, over and out, and Adam Spanker sucks both his thumbs," yelled Howie.

Freddy and Howie pulled the Jelly Leggers — which were small silver gadgets — out of their pockets, aimed, and fired at the legs of Adam and his gang. Instantly the boys all started walking crazy, their knees knocking together, their feet flopping around, like they had no bones in them.

Finally, they all fell down and flopped around on the floor like fish on a beach.

"Gotta love the old Jelly Legger," said Freddy.

"What is this stuff, magic?" screamed Adam.

"No, something far more powerful," said Freddy. "The human brain."

The jelly-leg effect finally wore off.

"Come on, men," shouted Adam. They surged forward after Freddy and Howie.

"You'll never catch us," taunted Freddy. He and Howie raced off.

"Spread out," ordered Adam. "We'll try and outflank 'em."

As he was sneaking through the barn, Adam got on his walkie-talkie. "Is Big Benny in place? Good. Wait until I give the signal. And get a hold of my Dad and tell him to get over here fast."

One of the gang turned the corner and stopped when he saw a pair of eyes peeking out from the hay.

"All right, come out of there," he ordered.

The small lump of hay rose up and walked toward him.

The boy pointed his paintball gun and laughed, "It must be little Howie Kapowie."

Suddenly the hay flew off and there was a yellow head that was swelling up like a balloon being pumped full of air. Ziggy let out an ear-splitting scream, "AAAAAGGGGGHHHHH!"

"That doesn't scare me," sneered the boy.

"Oh," said Ziggy in his tiny voice. "How about this?" He smacked himself on the head and his face, arms, and legs fell off.

The boy screamed and shot away so fast he ran right out of his shoes.

"Uh, guys," said Ziggy's mouth as it lay on the floor. "I need some help over here."

Another boy poked through some straw and

then froze when he saw a pair of red feet. Suddenly out of the straw popped Si with a big smile. "Hey, you looking at me?" he said, laughing.

Then Si disappeared and Meese popped up with his droopy face. "Hey, you looking at me?" he whined.

The boy's eyes grew bigger and bigger. Then both Si and Meese jumped in front of him and yelled, "RRRROOOOAAAARRRR."

The boy turned and ran.

Two other gang members got the jump on Curly.

"OkaycatchmeifyoucanbutIdon'thinkyoucan-sothere," mumbled Curly.

The two boys looked at each other. "Huh?" they both said.

Curly started running and they chased him. Curly looked back at them and started uncurling as he ran in circles while the boys tried to keep up. He was running so fast that the top of him came around behind the boys while the rest of him was still in front of them. He picked them up, running faster and faster in circles. Finally, Curly stopped and put the boys down. They were so dizzy they both fell over in a daze.

Another boy came face-to-face with Theodore. He pointed his paintball gun at him. "Hold it right there," ordered the kid.

"Young man," said Theodore in his deep, intellectual voice, "I seriously doubt that your parents would approve of this most distasteful conduct."

"What'd you say?" said the boy.

"Let me put it this way. In the grand scheme of things, what does your membership in this 'gang' do for your long-term prospects of getting a good education and finding gainful employment and becoming a productive member of society?"

"Huh?" exclaimed the boy. He aimed his paint-ball gun.

"Now I know you don't really want to shoot me with paint."

"Yes I do."

"Well, then you leave me no choice. I'll apolo-gize in advance."

Right before the kid pulled the trigger, Theodore stuck his finger in the barrel. The paint-ball gun fired backward and covered the boy in blue paint.

"A particularly beautiful shade, if I do say so myself," observed Theodore.

Meanwhile, Adam sneaked up behind Freddy, and pointed his paintball gun at him. "Hands up, Funkhouser. Now call all your freaky friends out here. I can't wait to march them into the police station. I'll be a hero."

Instead of surrendering, Freddy shot into the air using his anti-gravity flight belt.

"You can't catch me, Spanker," laughed Freddy.

"Whoops!" Freddy suddenly veered to the left and then to the right. He banged against one of the walls and then zoomed straight to the ceiling and slammed into it before he soared straight down.

"AAAHHHHH! Dad, I thought you fixed the flight belts," screamed Freddy as he plummeted. Howie was on the ground taking aim at Adam Spanker with his Jelly Legger when Freddy crashed into him, and both boys fell to the hay-piled floor. When they looked up, they saw Adam Spanker staring at them, his paintball gun pointed at them.

"Now, I've got you two dorks!"

Adam couldn't see it, but rising up behind him was something very big and very purple.

Freddy, who *could* see this, said, "Uh, Adam, I think you might want to get out of here." Freddy pointed behind Adam.

Adam slowly turned, and his eyes grew huge. Wally was standing there staring at him. He was so big his head was touching the barn's ceiling. He bent down so he was eye-to-eye with Adam and started sniffing him.

"Do you have any food?"

"NNN-OOOO," stammered a terrified Adam.

"Too bad, because that means I'm gonna have to EAT YOU!" Wally opened his enormous mouth.

Adam let out the loudest bloodcurdling scream that Freddy had ever heard and ran out of the barn so fast that he left most of his clothes behind. As they watched him, Si said, "Hey, he's wearing pink underwear."

Freddy turned to Wally. "Thanks, Wally."

"No problem, little dude."

Curly mumbled, "UhguysIthinkwehaveabig problemrightbehindus."

They all turned around and stared at what was coming right at them.

"Now you and your freaky friends are gonna get yours, Funky," yelled Adam Spanker. "Meet Big Benny."

Spanker's gang was rolling in the biggest paint-ball cannon that Freddy had ever seen.

Howie took a step back. "This doesn't look good, Freddy."

"I'm gonna cover you and your whole farm with a really special kind of paint, Funky: the kind that stinks and doesn't come off for at least a month," crowed Adam.

"I'm not afraid of you, Spanker," retorted Freddy.

"Oh yeah, why not?"

Wally answered. "Duh, because you're wearing pink underwear, dude."

Freddy, Howie, and the Fries all laughed.

Adam turned red. "Well, you won't be laughing for long. He turned to the gang members operating the cannon. "Ready?"

"No!" shouted Howie, who backed away.

"Aim," said Adam.

"Cease and desist immediately," commanded Theodore, but he backed up too.

To protect the others, Freddy threw himself in front of the cannon. But then he felt something grab him and toss him out of the way. He landed in the hay and opened his eyes right as Adam yelled . . .

"Fire!"

Big Benny roared and the huge paint cannonball exploded out and . . . and . . .

"NOOO!" Freddy yelled.

The cannonball flew right into Wally's enormous mouth. Everyone, including Adam and his gang, stood wide-eyed.

Wally stood straight up, took an enormous swallow, and they all heard the cannonball clunk right into his belly. Everyone kept watching as Wally smiled really big.

"MMMM. Me love whatever it was I just swallowed."

But then he gave a little shiver and his eyes crossed and he put a hand to his mouth.

"Uhh, Wally, are you okay?" asked Freddy.

"Not feeling too good, little dude."

Then there was an enormous explosion inside Wally's belly and it expanded six feet out in all directions.

"OOOOHHHH," said Wally. He bent over, rubbing his huge belly. "Feeling kind of like when I ate all those pies."

Freddy looked at Adam and his gang, who were still frozen, staring at Wally.

"Wally, you remember what made you feel better that time . . . ?"

"Good idea, little dudee-rudee. I know just where you're coming from."

Wally stood straight up, opened his huge mouth so that it was at least six feet wide, and aimed right at Adam and his gang.

Freddy yelled, "Fire!"

Compared to what came out of Wally's mouth at that instant, Big Benny seemed like a pop gun.

The entire Spanker gang screamed as one when the brown, sticky goop hit them so hard it blew them across the barn. They landed six feet off the floor and stuck against a wall, groaning and moaning. The entire barn stank!

"Boy, do I feel better," said Wally.

Freddy and his friends cheered triumphantly. But this was cut short by a shrill sound that drowned out their celebration.

Police sirens!

CHAPTER 17

PURPULIS ENORMOSIS

"Omigosh," cried Freddy. He peeked out the door and saw the red lights of the police car heading to the farm. "We've gotta get out of here." Freddy kicked Ziggy in the butt and he sprang back together. They all ran out into the rain and sprint-ed to the woods.

They finally stopped to catch their breath. The rain was pouring harder and harder, bouncing off them like beads. Freddy said, "Curly, go up and take a look."

Curly stretched up for a look around but quickly collapsed back down.

"Lightsinthewoodscomingthiswaybettergo," he mumbled.

"They're after us, keep moving," Freddy trans-lated.

They raced through the trees and then broke into the clear. Freddy stopped dead in his tracks. The Fries did too.

"This indeed presents a considerable conun-drum," said Theodore.

"You took the word right out of my mouth," said Wally.

"What word?" asked Ziggy.

"Coconutdumdum," Wally answered.

The raging river was blocking their escape.

"I've never seen it this bad," said Howie. "It must be all the rain. I bet the river's pouring over the dam."

"Is there a way around it?" squeaked Ziggy, wiping the rain out of his big eyes.

"No," answered Freddy.

"Well, do we have to cross it?" asked Si. "I bet there's a swell hotel right on this side of the river if we just head that way." He pointed to the right.

"The only thing that way," said Freddy, "is the dam. And we can't go to the left because Chief Spanker's back there. We're trapped."

Freddy looked at Curly. "How close are they?"

Curly stretched up in the air and then came back down. "Rightbehindus," he mumbled.

"Oh, that's just great," said Freddy angrily. "Now they're gonna find us and then they'll arrest my dad because they'll think he lied when he said he didn't know anything about you Fries."

Theodore said, "Freddy, it'll be okay. We'll think of something; at least I think we will."

"Yeah," added Si, "and when we do it'll be something terrific, you can bet on it, kid. Right, Meese?"

"They're going to put us all in jail and throw away the key," moaned Meese. "We'll never breathe free air again."

"I can't believe I messed up so badly," said Freddy. He started to sniffle and rub his eyes. Howie put his arm around his friend and started to sniffle too. "Well, at least it'll be over soon," added Freddy tearfully.

The footsteps grew closer. They could see the beams of the flashlights cutting through the trees.

And then Wally rose up and asked, "Hey, kid, you wanna get out of here?"

Freddy looked up, bewildered.

"What are you talking about, Wally? It's hopeless," said Theodore. "Even I can't think of anything."

"Well, I can."

"We can't eat our way out of this," said Ziggy. "So what can *you* do?"

Wally looked very determined. "They don't call me *purpulis enormosis* for nothing, little papoosie."

Wally opened his mouth and took a huge breath. Rain, leaves, and parts of trees were sucked in, and then the big purple Fry started to grow and grow and grow some more. Then he lay on the ground and started widening and flattening out. Then he curled up the edges of himself.

When he was done he said, "Okay, Theodore, stand right here —" Wally pointed to a spot that was near his flattened head "— and stretch your-self as high as you can."

Theodore did so.

"Okay, Ziggy, make yourself really wide and climb up on Theodore's shoulders."

"I don't think I can, Wally."

"Sure you can. All Fries based on nanotech-nology can morph," said Wally.

Ziggy took a deep breath, held it, and immedi-ately started getting very flat and very wide, like a big yellow blanket.

"Okay, Curly, wrap one end of yourself around Ziggy and Theodore so they're held together, and then hook your other end to both my arms, like this." Wally motioned what he intended Curly to do. The green Fry quickly did so.

"Okay, Si and Meese, over here." Wally pointed to a spot near the rear of his flattened body. "Okay, stick your legs in my belly button, but no tickling." Si and Meese stuck their legs through the hole and they popped out the other side of the flattened Wally. Then the purple Fry tightened his belly but-ton around their waist. "Now hold up your hands."

Freddy and Howie were still trying to figure what Wally was up to.

"Okay, you two," said Wally, pointing at Freddy and Howie. "Come here and take a hold of Si and Meese's arms. Now, Si and Meese, when Freddy and Howie move your arms one way you move your legs the *other* way. Got it?"

"Got it!" they both said. Si and Meese looked at each other in surprise.

"Hey," exclaimed Si, "that's the first time we've ever agreed on anything."

Meese looked almost happy but then quickly turned gloomy. "I'm sure it'll never happen again."

"Wally, what are you doing?" said Freddy as he looked around at all the Fries in these very weird positions.

"I bet you can guess, little dude."

Freddy thought for a moment and then it hit him. "We're a boat!"

"You got it," said Wally.

Freddy said excitedly, "You're the hull, Theodore's the mast, Ziggy's the sail, Curly's the rigging, and Si and Meese are the rudder and ship wheel."

"And *you're* the captain and Howie's your first mate." Wally looked over his little boat and crew. "Okay, boys, here we GO!"

He lunged forward into the water. They were instantly swept downstream. Wally's face was barely out of the water. He looked up ahead. "Hard to port," he called out to Freddy and Howie. "That's to the left."

"Got it," said Freddy, and he and Howie turned Si and Meese's arm hard to the left. Si and Meese pushed their legs, which acted as the rudder, to the right and the boat moved to the left.

"Now to starboard," shouted Wally over the noise of the rain and pounding water.

The boys turned the wheel to the right. Si and Meese moved their legs to the left and the boat turned to the right.

"Hey, Wally," said Freddy, "how did you know how to make a boat and steer it?"

"There was a picture of one in the book you brought. And I . . . well, I accidentally ate some of the pages, so I guess it seeped into my brain."

"Which book?" asked Theodore.

"Something called *Moby Dick*. About a big fish."

"Oh my," said Theodore. "Wally, do you know that you devoured a true masterpiece of American literature?"

"Hey, I only eat the best, blue dude."

"Wally," cried out Howie, "we're heading right for the dam!"

"Well, shiver me timbers and don't poop on me poopdeck," yelled Wally. "Avast there ya swine, hoist the mainsail, batten down the hatches, rig the jig, mop the slop."

"That line is assuredly *not* in *Moby Dick*," said Theodore severely.

"Hey, the story needed some jazzing up," replied Wally.

"Wally, the dam is really getting close," yelled Freddy. As he looked up ahead he saw that the river had gotten so high that the water was pouring over the top of the dam.

"Uh, Freddy," said Wally, "what exactly is a dam?"

Theodore answered instead. "A dam is typically an enormous wall built out of concrete that is used to hold back huge quantities of water for myriad purposes."

Freddy added, "And if we go over it, we'll be plunged hundreds of feet down into a raging abyss of water and rocks."

"Clear something up for me, Freddio," said Wally. "Is this plunging-into-the-abyss-thing bad?"

"YES!"

Si said, "Well, I've always wanted to plunge into an abyss of raging water and rock. Sounds exciting."

Meese bopped him on the head.

"See," added Si, "Meese thinks so too."

"OhIthinkwe'reallabouttodie," mumbled Curly as he looked ahead.

Wally said, "Okay, I guess we're gonna have to go ahead and barely escape with our lives." He took a deep breath and yelled out, "Hard to port! And I mean really hard!"

Freddy, Howie, Si, and Meese pulled with all their strength, but the current was so strong that they kept right on heading toward the dam.

"This doesn't look good," cried out Howie as he

saw the water pouring over the dam. He pulled out all his cheese cubes and ate them. "Now at least I can die happy."

Theodore saw the big tree sticking over the river and, using his enormous microchip brain, came up with a plan.

"Wally," yelled Theodore, "grab that big tree now!"

Wally morphed out an arm, snagged the tree, and the purple Fry boat shot out of the water and into the air.

"Hold on, everybody," shouted Theodore.

They flew across the surface of the water, heading right for the dam. Wally's arm stretched and stretched. They sailed in the air over the dam, but right as Wally's arm was about to snap off, he leaned to the left as hard as he could and they swung around and crashed onto the other side of the river. The boat came apart, and everybody just lay there.

Finally Freddy said, "Wally, you saved us. You're a hero."

Wally didn't say anything. They all looked at him lying there, staring at the sky.

"Uh, Wally, are you okay?" asked Freddy.

"Got a problem, little dude," he said.

"Are you hurt?"

"Nope. Bigger problem than that."

"So what is it?" asked Freddy anxiously.

CHAPTER 18

THE SPANKERS STRIKE BACK

After hiding in the woods for most of the night, Freddy, Howie, and the Fries made their way back to the farm very early the next morning while it was still dark. The police were gone, and so were Adam Spanker and his gang. But the barn still stank from Big Benny.

"I better get home before my parents miss me," said Howie. He took off.

Freddy and the Fries went back to Freddy's lab. "Okay, we have to get ready for the Founders' Day parade. Nothing can stop us now, guys. I need to help my dad and sister get ready."

"Can we come to the parade?" asked Ziggy.

"No, somebody might see you. But you've already helped rebuild the float. That's plenty."

When Freddy got to the farmhouse he was just about to sneak in when someone said, "Freddy, where have you been?"

He turned around and there was his father. Behind him and wearing a robe was his sister. She cried out, "We've been looking all over for you. We thought something had happened to you." Nancy hugged Freddy tightly, and he thought he even saw a small tear in her eye. Then she pushed him away and said, "The police were here, you little slug."

"The police? What did they want?" Freddy asked innocently.

"Something about a disturbance. They didn't find anything, but Chief Spanker looked very upset," said his father.

"Answer Dad's question, Freddy; where have you been?"

"I've been in my lab working on some special stuff for the parade today. I guess I lost track of time."

"A likely story," huffed his sister.

"Now, Nancy," said her father, "I've done the very same thing in my lab too. Okay, Freddy, go try and get some sleep. It's going to be a busy day today."

"Don't worry, Dad, we're going to win the competition," said Freddy.

"That's what I'm afraid of," replied Alfred.

"Huh?" exclaimed Freddy.

"Now that the Guacamole Brothers quit we don't have enough help to serve a lot of people. So if we win and the Burger Castle is packed, people won't have a good time and they probably won't come back. I've tried to get other people to help, but the Spankers have hired everybody in town who've ever worked in a restaurant."

His father and sister went off to bed with glum expressions while Freddy just stood there, stunned. *All that work, for nothing. Even if the Burger Castle float won, the Spankers were still going to get all the customers.* He looked out the window, toward where his Fries were hidden in the lab. And then it hit him. There was only one thing left to do.

Freddy waited until he could hear his sister snoring heavily. Then he crept into her room, grabbed all the costumes out of her trunk, and put them in a bag he had taken from his room. He opened the window and threw the bag out. Then he raced outside, grabbed the bag, and ran to his lab.

Later that morning the Funkhousers loaded up their station wagon and hitched the Burger Castle float behind it. They had covered up the float with a big sheet of blue tarp so it would be a surprise to the crowd.

On the way to town, Nancy kept going over and over her lines from Shakespeare.

"If chance will have me king, why, chance may crown me," she said in a deep, dramatic voice, quoting *Macbeth.*

"I'd like to crown you," said Freddy, "with a hammer."

She glowered at him and quoted from *Romeo and Juliet*, "I will be cruel with the maids. I will cut off their heads."

"Dad," complained Freddy, "Nanny Boo-Boo said she was going to cut off my head."

"That's nice, son," answered Alfred. "You two play so well together."

When they arrived in downtown Pookesville they pulled into the area where all the other floats were and unhitched their float from the car.

"Okay, Freddy," instructed his father. "Nancy and I will head over to the Burger Castle and get things ready. You stay here with the float. We'll be back in plenty of time for the parade."

After they left, Freddy quickly ducked under the skirting that ran along the bottom of the float. He opened the trapdoor that accessed the hollow insides of the Burger Castle.

"Hey, Fries, you okay in there?"

Six pairs of eyes stared back at him in the darkness.

"A-okay," said Si. "I love the dark. It makes me feel all cozy."

There was the sound of chattering teeth. "I . . . I . . . I'm scared of the dark," moaned Meese.

"Hey, I'm here to protect you," said Si.

"That's what I'm afraid of," replied Meese.

"Okay," said Freddy, "just stay in your hiding place. Once the parade is over, I'll sneak you into the Burger Castle. Got it?"

"Got it," said Theodore. "A remarkably vibrant plan you conceived, Freddy. Based on the Trojan Horse theory, of course."

"Hey, I was going to say that," complained Wally.

Freddy and the Fries couldn't hear Adam Spanker and his father slip over to the Burger Castle float and lift up a corner of the tarp covering it. Their eyes widened at the sight of it.

"I thought you said you destroyed their float," whispered Stewie Spanker to his son.

"I did, but they must've rebuilt it."

"We can't afford to lose the competition to these clowns," said Stewie. They heard a noise, and Stewie put the cover back down and said, "I'm going to go and get something to make sure we win. If Funkhouser's around when I get back, you distract him. Got it?"

"Got it, Dad." Stewie took off and Adam hid behind another float.

Meanwhile, Freddy closed the trapdoor and ducked back outside.

Howie came running up to Freddy. "I heard that Chief Spanker found Adam and his gang stuck to the wall of your barn. And they told him everything they'd seen. But they didn't have any real proof so he couldn't make an arrest. And Adam *was* trespassing on your property. But they're all here today and they're going to be watching for anything suspicious."

"That's just great." Freddy put a hand up to his nose. "What is that smell?"

He looked over and stiffened. It was Adam. His hair was all slicked back, and his skin was orange. He stunk worse than a room full of poop.

"So, I see you rebuilt that piece-of-junk float."

Freddy and Howie faced off with him. "Not only did we rebuild it," said Freddy, "but we're going to win!"

"Yeah, right! That'll be the day."

Howie held his nose. "Man, you really stink. And you might want to do something about that orange skin. You look like a big, fat carrot." Howie and Freddy laughed.

Adam made big fists. "Why you little twerp. Just wait until I find those monsters that attacked us last night. Then we'll see whose laughing."

"Monsters!" laughed Freddy. "Are you nuts?"

"Adam!"

They all looked up and saw Chief Spanker come around from the front of the Burger Castle float, where the tractor that was attached to it was located. He wasn't dressed as a policeman today. He had on his Patty Cakes outfit with a hat shaped like a burger and a cake. He looked like a big pink cow patty. He was carrying a small bottle that he quickly put in his pocket.

Chief Spanker stared at Freddy and pointed a fat finger at him. "I know something's going on here, and I'm gonna nail you and that crazy father of yours, Funkhouser." He turned to his son. "Come on, the parade's starting soon. We'll show these flunkies what a real float looks like."

"Right, Dad." Adam looked at Freddy and smiled. "So long, loser." Adam and his father exchanged a wink.

An hour later Alfred and Nancy returned, and the start of the parade was at hand. Alfred gave Freddy a walkie-talkie. "You'll be on the float with

your sister, waving to the crowd, but we can still communicate with these."

"Right, Dad," said Freddy. "Where is Nanny Boo-Boo?"

"She's on the float already, waiting for the great unveiling."

From the large reviewing stand set up on Main Street, Norman Thackery, the honorable chief judge of the Pookesville Court, and a fair and reasonable man — meaning he was no friend of the Spanker clan — announced the commencement of the parade.

Using a megaphone he said, "All float participants, start your engines."

Alfred was at the controls of the Burger Castle float. He called out, "Okay, Freddy, off with the cover."

Freddy pulled the cover off the float. And then his jaw dropped. There was his sister against the tallest turret of the castle, dressed in a long-flowing gown and a peaked hat, and she had tied herself with rope to the structure. She looked like a witch about to be burned at the stake.

"What are you doing, Nanny-Boo-Boo?" he cried out.

"You thought you were going to stop me from performing by taking out my balcony, didn't you, you little fiend? Well, I outsmarted the great brain this time."

"Get down! You're going to ruin everything."

"To be or not to be, that is the question."

"You're going to *be* a complete and total freak if you don't get down right now."

"Sticks and stones can break my bones, but little nerds can never hurt me."

Freddy stuck out his tongue at his sister and she immediately shot him a raspberry.

Freddy jumped on the float and they started off.

Freddy's walkie-talkie crackled. "Oh boy, look behind us, Freddy," said his father over the walkie-talkie.

Freddy's heart sank. Positioned right behind them was the Patty Cakes float. It was three times the size of any other float and built of new and costly materials. As Freddy had guessed when he'd seen it in the warehouse, it was a complete reproduction of the Patty Cakes Restaurant, complete with the Patty Cakes theme park, roller coaster, Ferris wheel, splash ride, movie theater, video arcade, and much more. All put together now, it was far more impressive than Freddy realized it would be.

Standing on the float was the entire Spanker clan, including Adam, outfitted in their best clothes, although some of the family wore clothespins over their noses. Freddy could smell Adam from where he was standing. A huge loudspeaker attached to the float shouted out the Patty Cakes ditty: "Patty-cake, patty-cake, Spanker man, follow us, follow us to Spanker Land."

"Wow," said Alfred over the walkie-talkie, "their float's going to be hard to beat."

"That's because they can afford some big-shot to build it for them," Freddy shot back.

"It's okay, Freddy, I still have a good feeling about today. Okay, here we go! Hold on tight, Nanny Boo-Boo."

"It's Nancy!" she yelled from the top of the turret.

The parade started off. All the floats in one long line glided down Main Street, passing in front of the reviewing stand where Judge Thackery would pick the winner.

The Burger Castle started off smoothly, but then the engine started sputtering.

"Something appears to be wrong," said Alfred.

Up on top of the turret, Nancy was really getting into her performance.

"Hark you, Guildenstern, and you too, at each ear a hearer — that great baby you see there is not yet out of his swaddling-clouts," she said in a deep voice while making many hand gestures.

One of Adam's gang called out to her from the crowd. "What are you supposed to be, a gargoyle?"

Nancy's face grew red, but she continued, "Happily, he is the second time tome to them, for they say an old man is twice a child."

Another gang member yelled, "Hey, maybe if we're lucky, lightning will strike and shut her up!"

Nancy took a deep breath and kept going, though her cheeks were very pink now. "I will prophesy he cometh to tell me of the players; mark it."

The first gang member hooted, "What is this junk?"

Nancy finally stopped and screamed, "It's *Hamlet,* you little moron."

Just then the Burger Castle float took a sudden jolt and died. As Alfred stared in perplexity, bubbles started coming out of the engine.

The Patty Cakes float passed them on the left. As it went by Adam grinned at Freddy. Adam called out, "Oh, and just so you know, any float that doesn't pass by the reviewing stand is automatically disqualified."

Alfred and Freddy looked at the engine. Alfred snagged one of the floating bubbles and took a sniff. "It seems that someone poured a bottle of shampoo into our gas tank," he said.

Freddy looked back at Chief Spanker. *That bottle he'd been holding!*

Adam yelled, "So long, loser!"

"What's going on, Dad?" asked Nancy.

"I'm working on it, Nanny Boo-Boo."

"For the last time, it's *Nancy!* Now where was I? Oh, right. 'O Jephthah, judge of Israel, what a treasure hadst thou!'"

"Treasure this," called out one of the Spanker gang as he nailed Nancy with a soggy tomato, right in the nose.

Freddy watched as his sister was getting bombarded, as his father worked on the sabotaged gas tank, and as the Spanker float drew ahead of them while the crowd cheered. It would be over for the Burger Castle. They would have to leave Pookesville. The Spankers would win.

And yet right in the middle of it all something clicked in Freddy's big brain. The fight was not over yet. He grabbed his father's walkie-talkie from the tractor cab and raced to the float.

CHAPTER 19

THE FLOAT THAT REALLY FLOATS

Freddy opened the trapdoor underneath the Burger Castle float and stuck his head through the opening.

"Fries, we've got a problem," he said.

"I know," said Ziggy; "we're not moving."

"Spanker sabotaged our engine, and unless we do something they're gonna win the competition," explained Freddy. He looked at Si and Meese. "Okay, guys, you know how when you hold your breath it turns to helium? Well, we're gonna use that little talent right now." Freddy handed a walkie-talkie to Theodore and quickly explained his plan.

Everyone put their hands together and said, "One Fry for all and all Fries for one, plus Freddy."

Freddy came out from under the platform, jumped in the driver's seat of the tractor, and said, "Uh, Dad, you might want to move back."

Alfred looked up from the tractor's engine, bewildered, "What was that, son?"

"Hey, get that float out of here!" shouted all the people on the floats lined up behind the Burger Castle.

"Hit it," yelled Freddy into his walkie-talkie.

Inside the Burger Castle float, Si and Meese took twin enormous breaths, filling up their hollow insides. After five seconds the air inside them turned to helium, the same gas used to fill balloons and make them fly. Inch by inch, the Burger Castle float began to rise into the air.

The crowd along the streets watched, mesmerized, as the float rose above their heads. Nancy, thinking that the crowd was mesmerized by her performance, smiled and said, "Thank you my fans, an encore? Well, if you insist." After taking ten bows in a row Nancy Funkhouser—still oblivious to the floating float—started reciting favorite movie lines. "Here's looking at you, kid," she said. "Play it again, Sam." She winked and exclaimed, "Rosebud!" She spread her arms to the sky. "Oh, Toto, I don't think we're in Kansas anymore."

But when she finally looked down and saw how far up she was, she started screaming.

Alfred wiped his hands on a rag, adjusted his glasses, and smiled.

"Go, Freddy," yelled Howie from the crowd. He was so enthralled by what he was seeing, he actually stopped nibbling on a cheese cube.

Freddy steered the float to the left and then to

the right. "Okay, Wally," he said into his walkie-talkie, "full speed ahead."

Wally put his mouth against a back window in the float and blew out an enormous breath. The float shot forward. Pilot Freddy Funkhouser knew exactly what his target was, and it was dead ahead.

"Okay," said Freddy into his walkie-talkie, "Let out half of your air."

Si and Meese instantly did so, and the float went into a nosedive.

Nancy, hanging on to the turret for dear life, screamed, "What is going on, Dad?" She managed to turn around and saw Freddy at the controls.

"Freddy Funkhouser, you put this float back on the ground this instant."

"That's where I'm going, Nanny Boo-Boo."

"Oh, all right, then. AAAGGGHHH!!!"

Wally had let out an enormous burp and the air force had knocked the Burger Castle sideways and then nearly upside down.

"My bad," Wally admitted sheepishly.

However, the crowd cheered wildly at this maneuver. Freddy smiled. "Okay, let's give them a show, guys! Back up!" he barked into his walkie-talkie.

Si and Meese filled themselves with air again.

The float soared into a vertical climb as the crowd watched in awed silence, all heads uplifted to the sky. The only sound was the hysterical

screams of Nancy Funkhouser. Freddy barked commands to the Fries, and Wally and the other Fries raced around the insides of the Burger Castle float, blowing air out different windows.

After a series of loop-the-loops, roller coaster plummets, and other stunts that rivaled the best of any barnstorming pilots, Freddy set his sights once more on his original target: the Patty Cakes float.

"Okay, reduce altitude and full power, guys."

Si and Meese let out their breaths as fast as they could and Wally blew as hard as he could out the window.

The Burger Castle float went into a tight dive, aimed right at the Patty Cakes behemoth. The Spankers saw what was coming, and they all started scrambling off the float. Adam Spanker looked so scared that Freddy actually felt sorry for him.

Okay, Freddy thought, *if I bust up the Spanker float, I'm as bad as Adam is.* He barked into his walkie-talkie, "Hard to port and then come in for a landing."

Right at the very last instant, the float went into a sharp turn and buzzed right by the Patty Cakes float. The Burger Castle float made a perfect landing directly in front of the reviewing stand to the cheers of the crowd.

Stewie Spanker was so angry by this that he

kicked the machine that was blasting the Patty Cake ditty and knocked it over. It kept playing, in a long moan that sounded like, "Poopy kook, poopy kook, spank me, man," before dying out completely.

Freddy climbed out of the cockpit and waved to the cheering crowd. Judge Thackery beamed down at him from the reviewing stand. "I think we have our winner," he said.

Alfred Funkhouser came running up while Nancy untied herself and climbed down from the turret, boiling mad.

"Freddy, I'm going to kill you," she shouted.

Freddy said, "But Nanny Boo-Boo, we won, we won!"

"What!"

"WE DID! WE DID!" shouted her father as he picked up Nancy and swung her around before setting her back down.

Nancy turned and saw the crowd cheering her and her family, and she immediately started smiling and waving. "Thank you, my loving fans," she murmured. "Another encore? Well, if you insist."

The Funkhousers were up on the reviewing stand and about to accept the award from Judge Thackery when the Spankers stormed up.

"This is outrageous," sputtered Chief Spanker. "Floats can't fly. They obviously broke the rules. You have to disqualify them."

"Oh yeah? Well, you sabotaged our float by putting shampoo in our gas tank," Freddy shot back.

Chief Spanker tried to look innocent. "I don't know what you're talking about. Adam, do you know what he's talking about?"

"No, father, sir," answered Adam politely.

"There," roared Chief Spanker. "It's this juvenile delinquent's word against ours, Thackery. So you have to believe us."

The Judge was thinking about this when Freddy spotted in the crowd the big-shot designer from New York he'd seen at the warehouse.

"Hey, that was a great float that you built for the Spankers," said Freddy so loudly that Judge Thackery could hear.

"Thank you very much," said the man. "They paid me a lot of money to do it."

Judge Thackery looked at Chief Spanker. "Is that true?" he asked.

The Chief began to sweat. "Well, um, he, uh, I, uh . . ."

The judge said, "The rules specifically state that each float must be entirely designed and built by the people entering it. No paid outside help is allowed." He turned to the crowd. "The Spanker float is disqualified and I hereby declare the Burger Castle float the winner."

A mighty cheer went up through the crowd.

Judge Thackery looked at Alfred Funkhouser. "Alfred, I know you're a very brilliant scientist,

but how in the world did you get that float to fly?"

Alfred looked at his son. "I'm not the only scientist in our family, Judge. But if I had to guess, I'd say it was a simple matter of physics — right, Freddy?"

Freddy beamed.

But as Freddy and his family accepted the first-place trophy, Adam Spanker was already plotting something to turn defeat into victory.

CHAPTER 20

THE BURGER CASTLE'S A HIT

Freddy flew the Burger Castle float over to the real Burger Castle as fast as he could, while his father and sister followed in their car. Freddy had a lot to do before anyone got there. As he looked down from the air he saw hundreds of people streaming toward the Burger Castle for lunch.

When his father and sister pulled up in their car, Freddy had already gotten the Fries in the back entrance and led them to a room with clothes lockers. He opened the locker doors and pulled the costumes out.

"Good thing these costumes are made of rubber, so they'll stretch. But I have to make a quick modification on Si and Meese's. I brought some stuff to do that."

Five minutes later Freddy was finished. "Okay, you know what to do. Meet me at the front entrance in five minutes."

Freddy hurried off to find his dad and sister.

Alfred had his tomato costume on and was warming up the ovens and getting the fat-free fry machines popping. Nancy went flouncing by in her ketchup costume.

"Dad," she said, "how can we possibly serve hundreds of people for lunch?"

"We'll manage somehow," said her father.

"Uh, Dad," said Freddy. "I found some people to take the Guacamole Brothers' place."

"What! Who?"

"Some friends of mine."

His sister said, "I didn't think you had any, except for that cheese cube nerd, Howie Kapowie."

"Where are they?" asked Alfred.

"Here we are," boomed out a voice.

They looked over and saw the five — six if you counted heads — bodies coming toward them.

"They're dressed as fries," said Nancy.

"That's right. They're wearing the Guacamole Brothers' costumes," explained Freddy. "Well, with a few modifications."

The Fries stopped in front of them. They each were dressed as regular-looking French fries with zippers down the back. Wally was squeezed so tightly into his that it looked like it might burst open any second.

Nancy looked at Si and Meese closely. Their costume had been modified to allow for the two heads.

"You have two heads," said Nancy.

"Duh, they're Siamese twins, Nanny Boo-Boo," said her brother.

Si said, "Or as we like to say, conjoined."

Alfred was looking at Theodore, who had put his glasses and bowtie on the outside of his costume. Freddy suddenly remembered that the glasses and bowtie used to belong to his father. Alfred rubbed his sharp chin while Freddy and the Fries held their collective breaths. Finally he said, "Freddy, they're perfectly perfect. I've never seen better specimens. They must be very special fries."

"Oh, they are, Dad, they are," answered Freddy, letting out a sigh of relief.

"Well, thank you," said Alfred. "Now I guess we better get to work."

When the lunch crowd started piling in, the Funkhousers could only stare at the masses for a few minutes.

"Wow," said Freddy, "so this is what it's like to have customers."

Alfred looked a little intimidated with all the hustle and bustle, but then he rubbed his sharp chin and said, "Okay, let's serve these people some good food for a change."

The Fries plunged right in, cooking food, carting dishes, and serving the customers.

One little boy tugged on Wally's arm.

"Hey, mister," he said. "You're the biggest fry I've ever seen."

Wally got down on one knee and patted the kid on the head. "I'm what they call super size, little dude. Put her there." They high-fived.

The little boy held up a French fry. "Want one?"

Wally recoiled back. "Sorry, little dude, I can't eat my own kind."

As Wally was walking back to the kitchen, Ziggy stopped him.

"Are you all right, Wally? You don't look so good."

"I can't believe it, little dude."

"Can't believe what?"

"I just turned down food."

Later, the Fries performed for the crowd. Using Theodore as a bat, Wally would hit Ziggy up in the air and Curly would run and catch him. The crowd roared. Si and Meese were also a big hit. Si would laugh really loudly whenever someone tickled him, while Meese would bawl on cue.

Freddy watched and laughed along with everyone else. But then he stopped laughing. Coming in the door was Adam and his gang. And with them was Chief Spanker, dressed in his police uniform now, along with Judge Thackery, a reporter, and photographer from the *Pookesville Tattler* newspaper.

CHAPTER 21

THE FINAL SHOWDOWN

Adam walked very confidently over to Freddy. Alfred Funkhouser came out from the kitchen. Nancy watched from the corner, her arms folded over her chest while all the Fries gathered together and looked on nervously.

"Okay, Funkhouser," called out Chief Spanker. "We're here to arrest you."

"Arrest me? For what?"

Everyone in the Burger Castle stopped eating to listen.

Judge Thackery stepped forward. "I'm sorry, Alfred, I'm sure this is really all sour grapes on Spanker's part, but Adam claims that your son and his friends shot them with giant fruits and vegetables while flying through the air, made their legs turn to jelly, and had them chased by monsters. And lastly, they were stuck to the wall with smelly, stinky stuff."

All the customers started laughing at this. Adam would have turned beet red if he weren't already a stinky orange.

The Judge continued, "Now it wasn't just Adam. All the boys here said the same thing. They saw monsters."

"Monsters?" repeated Alfred. "We don't have any monsters on our farm, do we, Freddy?"

"I've never seen any monsters on our farm," said Freddy, "Except for Adam last night."

Adam lunged forward. "Why you little —"

Judge Thackery grabbed him. "Now we'll have none of that, Spanker."

"Judge, I don't know what to tell you," said Alfred. "But we don't have any monsters."

Adam was looking at the Fries and pointed a fat finger at Wally. "There's the monster, right there."

Everyone looked at Wally.

"See, he's a French fry," said Adam excitedly. "And so are the rest of them," he added, pointing at the other Fries.

"Good grief, they're in costume," exclaimed Freddy.

"I'm telling you that these are the monsters I saw last night!" yelled Adam.

"These are Freddy's friends who came to help us at the Burger Castle today," said Alfred. "There's not a monster in the bunch."

"Well, there's an easy enough way to resolve this," said Judge Thackery. He pointed at the Fries. "Fellows, go ahead and unzip your costumes and show everyone that you're not monsters."

The Fries looked at one another. Nancy Funkhouser kept her arms folded over her chest and watched closely.

"Come on, fellows," prompted the Judge.

"Right, go ahead, fellows. It's okay," said Alfred, "we have nothing to hide."

The Fries still made no move to take off their costumes.

Nancy went over to Freddy and whispered fiercely, "Congratulations, you idiot. We'll lose the Burger Castle, dad will go to jail, and we'll be out on the street."

"Shut up!" whispered Freddy fiercely. But he turned to the Fries with a defeated expression. "It's all right, guys, take off your costumes."

The Fries looked at one another and shrugged. Ziggy went first, unzipping his fry costume. When it hit the floor Adam shouted, "See!" And then he froze.

Ziggy stepped out of his costume and came forward. He had pale skin and dark black hair fashioned in a pompadour. He wore jeans, a plaid shirt, and tennis shoes.

Theodore undressed next and stepped forward. He wore a college sweater, khaki pants, and suede shoes. His hair was long and blond and he still wore his glasses. His skin was even paler than Ziggy's.

After that it was Curly's turn. He wore a bulky football jersey, his ball cap, sweatpants, and high-top basketball shoes. His skin was pale too, but with a greenish tinge.

"He has a cold," explained Freddy.

Next, Si and Meese came out of their costume. They both had blonde hair and wore an orange jumpsuit and work boots. Their skin was very tanned.

"They work outside a lot," said Freddy.

"It has two heads," exclaimed Chief Spanker.

"They're Siamese twins, Spanker," said the judge angrily.

"Or 'conjoined,' as we like to say," Si commented.

Finally, big Wally took off his costume. Everyone gasped. Wally was wearing a long-sleeved flowered cotton dress that, fortunately, went down to his ankles. He had big red hair, huge eyelashes, and his feet were mashed into high heels.

Judge Thackery finally pulled his gaze away from Wally and tapped Adam on the shoulder. "Do you know that it's illegal to file a false police report, Spanker?" said Judge Thackery testily as he gazed first at Adam and then at his father. "You can go to jail for that," continued Judge Thackery. "I want you both in my courtroom first thing Monday morning, and I'll decide your punishment."

Freddy watched as, one by one, Adam's gang slipped out the door and ran away. Chief Spanker drew Alfred to the side. "I'll get you for this, Funkhouser, if it's the last thing I do."

Adam grabbed Freddy and said, "You're dead, Funky."

Something hit him from behind and spun him around. Freddy thought for sure it was one of the Fries, but it wasn't. It was his sister.

"Here, you big ape, try this." Nancy pulled out a pill slinger and shot a capsule into Adam's mouth. Unable to help himself, he swallowed it and immediately turned green.

He grabbed his throat. "You've poisoned me!"

"No, it's just a little burp pill. Oh, excuse me, I mean a little pooper pill."

Adam's face scrunched up and he balled his fists, but then he gulped, his eyes grew very big, and he took off running and screaming, "I need a bathroom!"

"Son," yelled Chief Spanker. "You come back here." He took off running too while the *Pookesville Tattler* photographer snapped their picture.

As soon as they were gone, everyone in the Burger Castle started cheering. Wally lifted Freddy onto his shoulders and paraded around with him.

The reporter came over to the Funkhousers.

"The story'll run tomorrow. It should help your business." He looked around at the happy crowd munching away. "Although it doesn't look like you need any help with that."

Alfred joined Freddy and said, "I want to hire your friends to work here full-time." He paused and added, "You never did tell me their names."

Freddy pointed to them as he said their names: "Ziggy, Theodore, Si, Meese, Curly, and Wall — I mean, Wilma."

"Perfectly perfect. They make the best fries I've ever seen. Why, it was like they were born for the role."

"Dad, you have no idea."

Alfred Funkhouser started to walk off and then turned back and said in a low voice, "Oh, Freddy, go ahead and give your sister back her costumes. I'll get some other clothes for the Fries so people won't find out what they really are. And they can live in your lab until we figure something else out. Who knew that nanotechnology combined with my super-secret potatoes would have such an interesting application."

As his father walked off smiling, Freddy reminded himself that his dad was the smartest person he knew.

Just then Freddy felt a poke in his back. He turned around to find his sister staring at him. "Thanks for helping me out with Adam," he said.

"Well, I just wanted you to know that while I still think you're a little brat, what you did was, like, really...cool." She smiled for an instant before scowling. "And if you tell anybody I told you that, I'll cream you!"

She flounced off, but without saying "Hmmpphh!" or even "Deee-ssssgggusting."

Freddy couldn't believe it. Had his sister just said something nice to him?

After closing up, Alfred and Nancy drove the station wagon back to the farm. Freddy wanted to walk home with his friends. They came out of the Burger Castle still dressed in their clothes and makeup.

Wally looked down at the moat. "Is that ice cream down there?" he asked, smacking his big lips.

"No, it's a Vroom shake my dad makes. This month's flavor is tangerine marmalade."

"MMMM. Me love tangerine marmalade." Then Wally made a face. "Ouchie-oochie!' as he teetered around on his high heels. "How do people walk in these things?"

"How do you like wearing a dress, Wally?" asked Ziggy.

"A dress!" exclaimed a horrified Wally. "I thought this thing was a food bib."

"And your name is Wilma, at least at the Burger Castle," said Freddy.

They crossed the drawbridge and Freddy hit a button on his remote control to raise it.

"I want to thank you guys for all you've done," said Freddy.

"Well, that's what friends are for," said Si. "And we're the happiest friends you'll ever have."

"Speak for yourself," whined Meese.

"You know, at first I just wanted to help my family by inventing you guys," admitted Freddy. "And then I forgot about that and I just wanted to be rich and famous."

"And now?" asked Theodore.

"And now, I'm just glad that we're all friends together, even if nobody else knows what you really are." He put out his hand. "All Fries for one and — wait a minute, where's Wally?"

Then they heard an enormous splash. Freddy and the others were instantly drenched by a huge wave of something.

Freddy sputtered and swallowed some of the stuff. "Tangerine marmalade! Oh no, don't tell me he —"

"Yep," mumbled Curly, "He'sintheredrinking-themoat."

"WAALLY!" they all yelled, and jumped in after him.